STOLEN

A DARKISH PARANORMAL FANTASY ROMANCE

C.D. GORRI

C.D. GORRI

STOLEN

Lords of Nightfall

Book 1

by C.D. Gorri

Edited by BookNookNuts

DEDICATION

For the readers who dream of dark wings, stolen vows, and dangerously beautiful monsters who'd burn the world to claim their mate.

You know exactly what kind of story this is.

And you want it anyway.

This one's for you.

-C.D.

LORDS OF NIGHTFALL

Kidnapped by Demon Princes.
Thrust into a realm of shadows and seduction.

These curvy human women were never meant to set
foot in Nightfall, a land ruled by ruthless Demon
Lords and bound by blood-oaths, ancient power,
and a crumbling prophecy.
But fate, or something far darker, has brought them
here.
Each woman is claimed as a fated mate, their bodies
and magic the final hope to restore a dying world.
The Princes demand loyalty, obedience, and passion.
The women agree to play the role of devoted mates
to stay alive. To buy time. To find a way home.
But the rules of this realm are twisted.

The longer they remain in Nightfall, the deeper the bond becomes.

The more they pretend, the harder it is to remember they were pretending. And falling for a Demon? It's the most dangerous risk of all.

Because if their human hearts betray them, they risk losing more than their freedom. They'll lose their very souls.

One rule could save them, if only they can remember it:

Nothing is as it seems in Nightfall.

Series Titles:

Stolen

Taken

Broken

Saved

STOLEN

He needs her to claim the realm that should have always been his.

Jules

I always wanted to belong, but I never meant to belong to him.

Bartending in a dive across the river from the city isn't all it's cracked up to be. One night, after a scuffle with rowdy customers, a stranger named Alaric steps in.

He's no ordinary man—dangerously beautiful and skilled in combat. After saving me, he asks a simple question.

Are you alone in the world?

I answer honestly, but it's a mistake.

Alaric kidnaps me to another realm, where I'm the only human and prey in a harsh, unforgiving world. He needs me as his mate to claim his destiny, and I'm powerless to resist. His charms are impossible to fight, and as long as I stay loyal, I'll be safe. *But how can I stay with someone whose hunger for power outweighs his need for me?*

Alaric

Claiming the throne of Nightfall was always my destiny.

But to do it, I need a mate.

Willing or not.

Jules is human, but the blood in her veins calls to mine like no other. She's the key to my crown, the only one who can anchor my power and secure my claim. I didn't expect to crave her the way I do.

Her fire. Her stubbornness. Her softness that hides a strength I never saw coming.

I brought her here to use her. To bind her to me with ancient rites and magic older than the realm itself. But now? Now I would burn kingdoms to keep her.

The realm needs a ruler. But my heart has already chosen a queen.

WELCOME TO NIGHTFALL

In a hidden realm layered just beyond the human veil, chaos is brewing, and its tremors are already echoing through the worlds we know.

Nightfall is one of many planes of existence in the vast, interwoven tapestry of the universe. It is a land of raw magic and unbreakable laws, a realm where dreams are not just fleeting whispers in the night, but living forces threaded into the minds of sentient beings to shape civilizations, inspire wonders, and birth empires.

But for every dream, there is a nightmare. And in Nightfall, nightmares take form.

Those who worship the dark are SoulTakers, and like everything else they have a purpose.

But it is the Lords' duty to ensure the realm is protected at all times.

Balance is sacred.

But where there is wonder, there must be wildness. Where beauty blooms, savagery follows.

To hold it all together, a steady hand is needed.

Unyielding, brutal, wise.

That hand belongs to the Prime—the ruler of Nightfall.

But the old Prime is dead.

Struck down by a devastating ambush from the SoulTakers.

These interdimensional parasites devour dreams, feed on desire, and leech the magic from every realm they touch.

Nightfall is unraveling.

Its magic is flickering.

Its borders thinning.

Its people, frightened and fractured.

With the Prime gone, there is no order.

No shield. No anchor.

Only four Lords remain.

Elemental, ancient, and Demon-born, each rules a dominion of Nightfall with terrifying strength.

Lord Alaric, Air—*a cunning shapeshifter with Dragon's blood and illusions sharp enough to cut.*

Lord Kael, Water—*ancient, cold, and deep as the oceans he commands.*

Lord Thorne, Fire—*blazing with rage and passion, feared by all but bowed to by none.*

Lord Dagan, Earth—*unshakable, dark-winged, bound to stone and storm.*

Bound by uneasy alliances and even older rivalries, these four must obey the one law that still holds power.

To rise as Prime, each must claim a fated mate.

But none of them believe in fate. None of them believe in love.

Instead, they plan to cheat the system, to trick the crown, the realm, even the Fates themselves. By finding the softest, most vulnerable hearts in the cosmos—*humans*—they'll attempt to forge false bonds strong enough to awaken the Prime's magic.

It's a dangerous gamble. But they are Lords of Nightfall. And they don't lose.

Yet as the SoulTakers draw closer, and the realm's edges begin to fray, one truth becomes clearer than ever before.

If they fail to unite, if the balance tips too far, if love is only a lie, then Nightfall will be destroyed.

And with it, every world connected to it.

Including ours.

PROLOGUE

ALARIC

The storm above us is cosmetic. I should know, *I summoned it.*

A touch of drama never hurts when four would-be kings are gathered to bicker like old crows.

Lightning flashes beyond the obsidian walls of the Eyrie, my personal stronghold at the edge of Nightfall's skyward border.

Below us, the realm churns with unrest.

I can see it in the haze of magic seeping into the atmosphere from all sides of the Endless Forest.

Nightfall is a place of mystery and magic. It is to be respected.

I learned that at the hands of the old Prime,

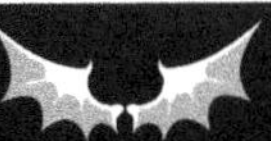

when I was barely old enough for my wings to carry me.

Fuck, I miss that old man. And I vow to have my vengeance on those who killed him.

The SoulTakers creep in closer with every passing day, and the seat of the Prime grows colder still.

With the absence of a Prime, the realm is vulnerable. Our people suffer. And up here?

We argue like boys in a schoolyard.

"Why are we here? What makes Alaric, Lord of Air, think he can summon us to his little kingdom like we're his servants?"

Thorne, Lord of Fire, frowns as he spits his venomous words. His flame-colored eyes flash with his anger, but I know he is every bit as sorrowful as I am about the fall of our Prime.

"You know, your bitter words don't make you a leader, Thorne," I say with a smirk, propping one boot on the ancient obsidian table. "They just make you more irritating than usual."

Thorne's molten eyes narrow. Fire dances along the edge of his skin, licking at the air like a warning.

"At least I don't hide behind trickery and illusions."

"Please," I scoff, spreading my hands. "Illusions are simply truths waiting for a good story."

Kael sighs from his side of the table, broad arms crossed over his sea-glinted armor. His horns catch the light when he shifts.

"You two are children."

"And you're a puddle with a crown fetish," Dagan mutters from his corner, wings folded tight as stone slabs behind him. "We're wasting time. The realm needs a Prime."

"Then go find a mate already and see if you can wear the crown," I say lightly. "Unless you're afraid the Fates won't fall for your brooding routine."

His almost pure white eyes meet mine, full of violence and contempt, but also—*amusingly*—a spark of worry.

Because we all know the same thing:

To claim the crown, we must be mated.

Not just joined.

But truly mated, and with all the blessings of the Fates themselves.

Only a pure matebond will awaken the crown, grant the Prime's magic, and keep Nightfall from tearing itself apart.

But who among us believes in true love?

Not Thorne, with his scars and fiery contempt.

Not Kael, with his ocean of regrets and submerged secrets.

Not Dagan, the stone-hearted executioner with his angelic appearance and Demonic ruthlessness.

And certainly not me.

Love is a myth.

A pretty lie.

But mating? That we can fake.

"Humans," I say, leaning forward, fingers steepled. "They're the key."

"Humans?" Dagan says the word like it's a curse.

"What are you on about? A *zareth* cannot be faked," Thorne scoffs.

"Wait a moment. Alaric might be on to something," Kael murmurs.

All of his attention is on me.

Of all the Lords, Kael and I get along the best. And judging by his smirk, he knows where I am going with this.

"Think about it for a second," I continue. "I don't speak of forging a real soul bond. Not a *zareth*, Thorne. Merely the *appearance* of one."

Everyone is silent. So, I press on.

"Humans have the softest hearts in any realm. Fragile. Loyal. Starved for affection. If we want to get past the crown's magic, if we want it to *think* we've found our true mates, we'll need to charm the Fates themselves."

Thorne scoffs. "You want us to seduce *mortals*?"

"I want one of us to win," I say, shrugging.

"Oh, I see. And we should all believe that you, *Lord Alaric*, would be content with any one of us wearing the Prime's crown?" Dagan turns his lips downward and growls.

"You can hear lies as well as I—"

"Yes, but you are the *Lord of Illusion*. You lie better than most," he interrupts.

"Do you dare impugn my honor in my own home, Lord Dagan?" I growl, feeling my magic spike alongside my temper.

"Brothers, please! We must remember ourselves. Without a Prime, our baser instincts vie for control. But we are better than that. Now, let's hear Alaric out," Kael says, standing and raising his arms in peace.

"*If* we can get a human to fall in love with us—"

"Wait like share one woman?" Kael asks, eyebrows raised.

This one. Always thinking with his cock.

I roll my eyes at him, fighting my smirk when the others do the same.

"No!" I snort. "Look, if each of us finds one

human woman and gets them to fall for us, and I mean truly fall in love with us, then maybe the crown won't know the difference. Maybe it won't care if we don't love in return. The Fates won't test us. They'll just *believe*."

Kael tilts his head. "And if we fail? If we bind ourselves to the wrong ones?"

Dagan answers, voice like grinding granite. "Then we die when the SoulTakers breach the gates, and it won't matter, anyway."

A heavy silence falls.

I break it, smiling with my inner Dragon showing himself through my eyes, always ready to play with his prey.

"Then we'd better hurry, brothers. It's a race now. First one to bring home a human and get her to say *I love you* wins the crown and rules the realm."

"And what happens when your mortal figures out the game? What if she finds out the truth and leaves you? What then, *Lord of Lies*?" Thorne asks.

I grin. "You just answered that question yourself. I am the Lord of Illusion, I lie better than anyone save maybe Satan himself. She won't know the truth. Not ever."

The four of us rise, old magic shuddering through the stones beneath our feet.

This is either the beginning of a new age or the end of it all—*of Nightfall, of everything.*

"Only one of us can ascend," Dagan begins.

"True, but all of us must try," I reply, placing my hand between us, palm down.

"Then we agree. We will all try this mad plan of Alaric's?" Kael asks with a wicked grin on his face.

Kael slaps his hand on mine, the strength in it echoes in the room.

His gesture is followed by Dagan, who claps his palm down on Kael's.

We all look to the last of us who has yet to agree.

It's Lord Thorne, of course. But he's always been an ornery bastard.

"Well, why the fuck not? Can't let this cocky prick have all the fun," Thorne mutters, tossing his hand on top of ours.

None of us plan to fall.

None of us believe in fate.

But we're going to try to cheat it anyway.

"May the best Lord win!"

CHAPTER 1
ALARIC

The human world stinks of metal and misery.

It's like this messy, repulsive, delightful cacophony of smells, and sounds, and sights that could make even the hardest Demon shiver in fright—or glory. Depends, I suppose.

I love it here.

There's something utterly intoxicating about the clutter of it all.

Neon signs flickering like dying stars, horns blaring, adding to the noise polluting the air, bodies packed too tight into streets slick with desperation, weeping with agony.

This realm is so noisy, so crowded—*so alive*. It

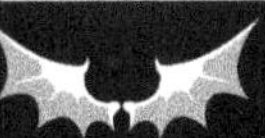

almost drowns out the thrum of magic beneath my skin.

Almost. But not quite.

I perch on the roof of a dilapidated warehouse across from a dive bar with a half unlit neon sign that's supposed to read *On the Waterfront Bar & Bites*.

Charming.

I've watched a hundred of these hole-in-the-wall establishments rot from the inside out.

But tonight?

Tonight, something different stirs in the air.

I can feel it.

See it stretch out in front of me the moment I pull the veil back with my magic.

A single thread.

Silver.

Spun tight with longing.

And it's hers.

That shimmering strand of fate winds through the ether like a tether, humming with emotion so sharp it could slice the skin if you touched it.

I've been watching it for days now, trailing behind her like a ghost she doesn't know she carries.

She's the one.

My human.

Pretty. Young.

Curves for miles and eyes that carry more story than she'll ever tell.

But more than that, *she's sad.*

Not broken. Not weeping.

No, her sadness is quieter than that.

It clings to her like fog at twilight.

Soft, lonely, and beautifully heavy.

It makes her vulnerable.

It makes her *perfect.*

Because sadness is a door.

And I know how to walk through it.

For now, I simply watch.

I drape my illusion over me like a well-cut coat.

Horns, wings, tail all tucked neatly into the folds of the metaphysical space that is Nightfall.

My true form steps into shadow, and the charming human exterior emerges, just tall enough to intimidate, just handsome enough to disarm.

And I wait.

My senses sharpen when the back door creaks open and she steps out into the alley, a heavy trash bag slung over one shoulder like she's carrying the weight of the world.

She works too hard.

I've watched her all week, clocking in at the bar

just before dusk, slinging drinks for entitled men and women who snap their fingers and stare too long.

She keeps her head down. Smiles too tightly.

Then walks home to that cramped little apartment with the chipped green door and the deadbolt she checks twice.

She doesn't know she's been seen.

That I've been following her scent through the city's filth. My inner beast, the Dragon who lives inside of me rumbles as he watches.

The creature has always been drawn to gold. And maybe that's what she is.

Valuable. Precious.

Tonight, she's grumbling under her breath, muttering about tips and trash and probably a few things I'd find entertaining if I wasn't already enchanted by the sound of her voice.

The door slams behind her, and she jumps a little.

Scared of the dark, Sweet?

No, that won't do. Still, I can teach her which things need fearing, which to respect.

One thing I can promise is that nothing will harm her while I'm around.

A rumble starts to build inside my chest, and I know my beast is on board with that.

She sighs and turns back, placing the lid on the dumpster.

A curl tumbles loose from her bun.

And her body—*gods, her body*—moves in those jeans like temptation made flesh.

Soft. Strong. Sinful.

I go very still.

Not because I'm surprised. I've seen her before, every night this week.

But because something changes.

Some deep instinct stirs beneath my skin, low and primal.

The kind of instinct that predates language.

It doesn't think. It just claims.

The back door swings open again behind her, the sound cutting through the alley like a warning bell.

She stiffens.

And I feel it.

Her pulse kicks, breath catching in her throat.

But this time, when her heart races, it's for a damn good reason.

She's not alone anymore.

Two men stumble into the narrow alley, loud

and careless, reeking of spilled whiskey and rotten testosterone.

I've seen them come in and out of the bar before, a couple of loudmouthed assholes with expensive shoes and cheap souls.

I slip deeper into shadow, every sense locked on her.

The silver thread between us hums so tight I can feel it in my bones.

This is the moment.

The moment.

I can barely make out her words as they corner her against the rusted dumpster, their voices low, slurred, and full of intent I have no patience for.

She raises a hand in warning.

Maybe to defend herself. Maybe to keep calm.

And then one of them reaches for her.

His hand brushes her cheek.

Casual. Presumptuous. Oily with entitlement.

Like she's his to grab, to frighten, to use.

I see it in his eyes. The way his grin turns feral.

He touches her again.

And something inside me snaps.

I don't roar. I don't growl. I don't announce myself.

But I move.

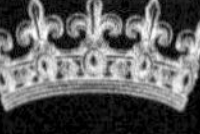

The air around me distorts as my magic pulses, dragging the shadows tight around my frame.

One second I'm watching. The next, I'm between her and them, a wall of rage dressed in the shape of a man.

The silver thread pulls taut.

Like it knows what's about to happen.

Like it wants this.

The man who touched her recoils too late. I reach out and grab his wrist, squeezing just hard enough to feel the tendons pop.

His knees give out. He gurgles something unintelligible. And his body cries out.

"Let me make something perfectly clear," I murmur, my voice like wind across a blade. "You've just made the last mistake of your life."

The man whose hand now hangs useless from his wrist doesn't even get a scream out. Not really.

I let go of his hand and give him a look—just a flicker of truth behind the illusion.

Just enough for him to see me.

To see the creature behind the eyes.

And he pisses himself.

"S-sorry," his buddy says.

"Wha-what are you?" he whimpers.

His friend is smarter than him. He shakes his

head and drags him away, stammering apologies I don't care to hear.

The two would-be attackers vanish into the night like rats scurrying from flame.

And now it's just me and her.

She hasn't moved.

Her eyes are wide, mouth parted. Staring at me like she's not sure if I saved her or stepped out of her darkest dream.

I don't speak yet. I just feel her.

The way her human soul hums like a struck bell.

The way the silver thread between us thrums with fate and fire and fear.

She's mine.

And I think she knows it.

And I know—*don't ask me how I know, I just do—* that she's going to answer me exactly the way I need.

Her big eyes sparkle as she takes me in from head to foot. This part is an illusion, but she doesn't know that.

I want to let it drop. I want her to see the real me. But I hold the veil up for a while longer.

"This isn't how I thought this would feel," I say aloud without meaning to.

"How you thought what would feel?" she asks.

I don't answer. I can't.

I'm still trying to process what's happening right now.

Mine.

I don't understand what this is. But I make the decision to take it.

To take her.

Whether the Fates meant it or not, I'm going to make this tiny human believe.

I'm going to make her fall for me.

But what if you can't?

I push the negative thought away. And even though my heart doesn't beat in the human sense, something inside me jolts.

Violent. Unfamiliar.

Recognizing.

Fated?

I don't think so.

I mean, is anything ever that simple?

I step forward silently, cloaking myself in the illusions I've mastered since before her ancestors learned to light fire.

She doesn't see yet. But me? I see everything.

The strain behind her eyes.

The shadows clinging to her like forgotten ghosts.

The heat in her blood.

She's human. Entirely.

And exactly what I need.

The rules are clear—*the first to find his fated mate and complete the bond becomes Prime.*

But no one said the mate has to know any of that.

Make her fall for you. Bind her to you. Pretend until the magic believes it.

That's the game.

And I'm very good at games.

I always win.

"Where did you come from?" she asks.

A crash of bottles from inside the bar startles her.

When she flicks her gaze back to mine—something happens.

Those wide, whiskey-colored eyes capture my attention like nothing else has in a millennium.

Still, I don't speak.

Not yet.

I let the air thicken between us like smoke.

Then, softly, I ask, "Are you alone in the world?"

I know the answer, but her verbal acquiescence is necessary to the magic.

Her lips part.

Confused. Curious. Slightly wary.

"Yes," she whispers.

Perfect.

The door swings open behind her, flooding the alley with light and the sharp scent of cheap beer and violence.

More drunken men stumble out, one already shouting.

Jules—*yes, that's her name, I know it now, like I know every piece of her*—flinches.

I've had enough interruptions. So, I step forward and let the illusion fall.

Seven feet tall, eyes glowing silver-blue, magic wrapping around me like a cloak of wind and intent.

"Go back inside," I growl at the humans.

They do. Without a word. Without under-standing why.

When I turn back to Jules, her breath catches, but she doesn't run. She blinks once, twice, like she's trying to wake from a dream.

"You should come with me," I say.

She hesitates. "Why would I do that?"

I smile.

"Because," I say, eager for reasons I'd rather not acknowledge, "I'm about to make all your dreams come true."

CHAPTER 2
JULES

This is not the life I wanted.

But it's the one I've got.

Another Friday night, another round of over-priced cocktails for Wall Street rejects with trust funds and zero personality.

I slide two tumblers of whiskey down the bar, plastering on a smile I don't feel as the guy who ordered them snaps his fingers at me like I'm a dog.

I don't flinch.

Not anymore.

That muscle's been dead a long time.

"Maybe smile more next time," he says, his

buddies laughing behind him like they're all part of some mediocre sitcom.

I'm already walking away, jaw tight, heart numb. If I don't move, I might say something I can't afford to. And I need this job.

It pays just enough to cover my shitty rent and my never-ending student loans for a degree I don't use.

Art.

What a joke.

My name's Jules, and I bartend in Hoboken for people who think suffering is when the bartender puts too much ice in their drink.

I've got no family.

No boyfriend.

No best friend.

Just a tiny studio apartment downwind of the old factories, and a sketchpad I don't touch anymore because looking at it hurts too much.

"Hey, Jules," my manager barks from the kitchen pass, "busboy called out. I need you to take on trash duty tonight."

Of course he did.

"Sure," I mutter, already grabbing the bag.

He wasn't really asking. The *or else* was implied.

I shoulder open the back door and step into the

alley, the warm summer night wrapping around me like the sigh of something tired.

The city buzzes just beyond the fence.

I can hear it. Feel it.

But it doesn't touch me. Not really.

I'm invisible here. And maybe I like it that way.

The bag splits as I hoist it toward the bin, bottles clinking loud enough to drown out my curse.

I yank the string tight and shove the mess down into the dumpster like it personally offended me.

Then I freeze.

There's someone there.

I can feel them watching me from the shadows.

Just watching. But still. It creeps me the fuck out.

My heart jumps into my throat.

You're being ridiculous, Jules.

I ignore it and bend to pick up what I've dropped.

The alley's always been gross—*hot, sticky, and stinking of rot and grease*—but tonight it feels worse.

Heavy. Like the shadows aren't the only things watching me.

I pause, the hairs on my neck standing up even though there's no breeze.

It's the strangest feeling.

Like I'm not alone.

Like somewhere someone out there is just waiting for the moment to jump out and say, *"hey there, I've been looking for you."*

Of course, there is no someone out there just waiting to claim me. I mean, reality isn't that kind or inventive.

I glance over my shoulder, unable to shake the feeling like someone is there.

Still nothing. Still no one.

Just the dim security light buzzing overhead and the usual city noise drifting in from the next street.

"Get a grip," I mutter, making sure I have all the garbage off the floor and inside the dumpster before I head back inside.

I'm not in any rush. The tips have been nil and the customers are cranky and rude.

I hate this job. But what else can I do?

I close my eyes willing that feeling of being watched to just go away.

But it lingers.

Like someone's breath on the back of my neck.

All night, I've had that crawling sensation.

Eyes tracking my movements, studying me.

Not in the way those barflies stare when they think I'm not looking.

No, this feels different.

Intense. Focused. Not leering. Searching.

I rub my arms and start to head back inside when the door bangs open again.

I freeze.

No.

Not them.

The two jerks from table nine—*Tony and Bobby or whatever their names were*—are stumbling into the alley like they've been waiting for a chance.

Loud. Laughing. Drunk in that smug, dangerous way some men get when they know nobody will stop them.

They'd been handsy all night.

One of them *accidentally* grazed my ass when I carried a drink to their table.

The other told me I had a *porn star pout* and asked what I did after closing.

My boss?

Please.

He told me to *smile more* and gave them free shots when they asked him when I was scheduled to work next, after I'd already told them *no*.

"Hey, sweetheart," one of them slurs, swaying closer. "Forgot to tip you."

"That's okay. Better get back inside," I snap,

trying to keep my voice even. "Bar's closing in twenty."

"Just being friendly." His hand reaches out, touches my face.

I frown and try to move away, but his friend is blocking the only exit.

His fingers grow bold, pressing firmly into my skin.

"Don't be a bitch."

Panic claws up my spine.

I try to yank free, but there's nowhere to go—cornered between the dumpster, the brick wall, and the two of them.

The sound of their derisive laughter makes me tremble with fear. I do not like this.

This is bad. Dangerous.

But then suddenly, *he's* there.

Not walking. Not running.

One moment it's just me and the assholes.

The next, this mystery man steps from the shadows like he owns them.

Tall. So tall. Broad shoulders, sharp jaw, something unearthly in the way he moves.

Graceful, but coiled with danger and power.

Like a predator on the edge of striking.

His eyes lock on mine, and the whole alley seems to still.

For a second, I forget the jerks who followed me out back with ill intentions.

I forget my name.

Hell, I forget how to breathe.

He's not just hot.

He's *other*.

Like from another world. Seriously.

And this is what I get for reading those sexy alien kidnapping books.

I mean, he's man, yes, but he's also *more*.

Like he was sculpted from shadow and smoke and made real just for this moment.

I don't even register what he does to the guy who touched me.

I just hear the pop of a wrist, the sharp gasp of pain, some exchanged words, and then they're both gone.

Fleeing without a backward glance.

And now I'm standing there, alone *with him*.

Only I don't feel afraid.

I should.

I know that.

But instead, my pulse is racing for another reason entirely.

Because whatever he is? My body responds before my brain can catch up.

And it wants him. Desperately.

Just breathe, Jules.

This strangely beautiful man saved me. But I don't know whether to thank him or run.

He's just *too much.*

Tall. Too tall.

Broad.

Too still. Frozen in his stance.

A statue carved from smoke and silver.

He steps forward, and the air shifts around him like it knows to get out of his way.

Dangerous.

But not in the way that makes me want to run.

Not in a way that reminds me of the jerks inside, or the creeps who wait too long outside the bar pretending they're looking for a rideshare.

No, this is different.

This is the kind of danger that pulls at something inside me.

A quiet voice that doesn't scream, *run.* Instead, it whispers, *watch.*

Wait.

Want.

He's not like the men I deal with every night.

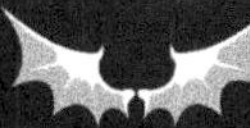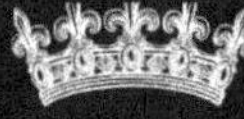

Hell, he's not like anyone I've ever seen.

There's something too perfect about him.

The way he moves. Like he's not bound by the same rules of motion the rest of us are.

Fluid.

Controlled.

Predatory.

That stupid question floats through my head, unbidden. You know the one.

Would you rather be alone in the woods at night with a man or a bear?

And every woman knows the answer.

Bear.

But this man?

Something about him tells me he could take on a bear and win.

With nothing but his hands and a calm, clinical sort of precision.

And the strangest part?

I still don't feel scared.

Because while everything about him says predator, nothing about him says threat.

Not to me.

In fact, for the first time in what feels like years, I feel seen.

Like I matter.

Something prickles at the base of my skull. A whisper of realization.

He's not normal.

Not even close.

There's a flicker of something in his eyes.

An unnatural glow, a depth that looks less like reflection and more like a window into another world.

A colder one. Older. More powerful.

And then he speaks.

His voice is deep and smooth. Rich like smoke and velvet, but with something steel-edged beneath it. Something sharp enough to slice through me clean.

"Are you alone in the world, Jules Strano?"

The question lands with terrifying precision.

Like he already knows the answer.

Like he's not asking out of curiosity, but confirmation.

I swallow hard. My throat is dry.

My mouth wants to lie.

But my soul answers for me, whispering *yes*.

I blink, frown, shake my head like I misheard him.

"I'm sorry. What?"

"Are you alone?" he repeats.

I should say no.

I should lie.

But I don't.

"Yes," I whisper this time out loud before I can stop myself.

The word hangs there.

True. Heavy. And something in his expression changes.

Like he's been waiting for it.

I take a step back. "Who the hell are you?"

He smiles. It's dark. Cocky. A wicked grin.

"My name is Alaric, and I'm going to make every one of your dreams come true."

And then everything goes dark.

CHAPTER 3

ALARIC

My entire being trembles when she says *yes*.

That single word slices through the veil like a blade.

It echoes in the space between us, and I feel it, My magic responding, swirling, claiming.

She doesn't even realize what she's done.

I step closer, slow and careful, not because I fear her, but because I don't want to rush the moment.

The silver thread between us tightens like a snare, humming with Fate's breath.

She blinks up at me, those wide, dark eyes soft with confusion, lashes trembling. A lamb in the mouth of the wolf.

But she doesn't run.

She trusts me.

Foolish girl.

Beautiful girl.

I reach for her gently, press two fingers to her temple.

My magic coils there, sinking into her skin with practiced ease.

She gasps.

Just a tiny sound.

So fragile. So precious.

Then her body goes limp and falls forward.

I catch her easily.

Soft.

She is unbelievably soft.

The moment I have her in my arms, the air begins to crackle. The veil stretches thin as spider silk, and then tears open in a slow, luxurious rip.

Magic surges like a tide, wrapping around us both, greedy and eager.

The tether is locked.

The crossing has begun.

I step through with my bundle—*my mate, my viyella*—cradled close, her breath feathering against my collarbone.

My plan is cemented in my mind like a spell inscribed in blood.

Charm her. Claim her. Use her to win the crown.

But there's something rising in me I didn't account for.

A flicker.

A whisper.

A feeling that maybe that this slip of a girl in my arms isn't what she seems.

She's human. Mortal. Ordinary.

She's supposed to be.

And yet, there's a resonance.

A warmth that doesn't come from magic.

A quiet hum that coils around my ribs and tugs tight like she already lives in the hollow parts of me I thought long dead.

It doesn't matter.

It can't matter.

I have a duty to the realm.

And this, lying to her, *creating the illusion of a devoted lover*, is the only way to see it through.

The veil parts for me, and I step across the threshold, determination rising like the north wind inside of me.

Entering Nightfall feels like diving under a waterfall.

The power of it all comes crashing over me,

familiar and fierce. The realm breathes beneath my boots, thick with magic and memory.

Here, my power unfurls just like my wings.

Here, I'm not just a creature playing mortal.

I'm me.

Alaric. Demon. Lord of Air.

She whines and I glance down, frowning.

The shift is always jarring for humans.

Their bodies resist, their minds twist in protest.

The realm changes the rules of reality, and their fragile senses fight against it.

But for me?

It's simply coming home.

I carry her through the stone halls of my keep, down the spiral corridor to the chamber I've prepared.

To my bed.

"Easy, *viyella*," I murmur, frowning.

The word for *mate* slips too freely from my tongue.

I ignore it, settling her atop the bedding.

She looks so pale and soft, shimmering like a silver star across the midnight colored blankets and sheets.

My magic stretches with a sigh, curling around us both like smoke seeking flame.

I breathe it in, holding her tighter.

Her scent is a balm in the storm.

Warm, light, and soft sweetness, threaded with exhaustion and unspent dreams.

Yes. She'll do. More than do.

I don't know why or how, but I feel something stirring.

Like something is shifting inside me, too.

And I can't tell if it's the realm, the magic, or her.

Nightfall always welcomes my return with shadows and silence. But now the air is thick with the scent of power and the weight of old magic.

I stare at her helpless to do otherwise and feel my loins stirring in response. It's unexpected. And so damn powerful, I almost groan aloud.

I don't mean to take her. Not tonight. Not yet. But I can't deny my attraction to her.

And the scent of her—*gods, the scent of her*—is already driving me mad.

Her cheeks are still flushed from the transition to this realm. Her dark curls are sticking to her skin.

I frown, noting her jeans are dirty and her shirt is splattered with cheap vodka and spilled beer.

That won't do.

I wave my hand, using my magic to remove her clothing and freshen her skin. I keep her modesty in place, hiding her luscious form beneath a silken sheet.

Fuck, she smells divine.

Like something mine.

I lean closer, inhaling at the curve of her throat.

Creamy. Warm. Sweet.

I nuzzle a little nearer, letting the scent settle into my bones.

Something animal in me purrs in response. My Dragon memorizing her already.

Then she stirs.

And I go still.

Her eyes blink open. Dark, rich, stunning. Confused, but not screaming.

Her voice is rough when she whispers, "Wha-what are you doing?"

I straighten just slightly, eyes locked on hers.

"What is that you smell of?" I ask, genuine curiosity in my voice.

She blinks. "It's body cream. Um, it has shea butter."

I hum. "It's lovely. Soft. It suits you."

She stiffens, trying to sit up, eyes wide when she realizes she is nude beneath the sheet.

"You undressed me?"

I nod.

"Do not worry, *Myrrin*. I didn't touch you."

Fuck. These terms of endearment keep spilling from my lips without so much as a by your leave.

"*Myrrin?*" she asks, putting the emphasis on the wrong part of the word.

"*Myrrin. MEER-in,*" I correct her pronunciation.

She cants her head to the side and says it again, correctly this time.

"*Myrrin.*"

I grin. Really, she is taking this much better than I thought.

"It means Sweet. Like your scent."

Her eyes widen before sweeping the room.

I watch her catalog everything—the stone walls, the flickering torchlight, the impossibly tall windows.

Then her gaze snaps back to me.

"Okay, why am I here? Where am I? And why am I naked?"

I take a breath. No more lies. Just not all of the truth.

"This is Nightfall," I say quietly, stepping closer. "You are naked because your clothes were soiled. And I've brought you here, Jules Strano, to be mine."

CHAPTER 4
JULES

I feel like I'm floating somewhere between sleep and waking.

The air smells like smoke and silk and something older than time.

There's no trash here.

No clinking glasses or shouted orders.

No sharp whistles or wandering hands.

Only stillness.

Only him.

He calls himself Alaric.

His voice came to me first. Low and velvet-wrapped, threading through the shadows of my mind like a lullaby meant for monsters.

Now it's like I can feel his presence before I see him.

The hum of him.

Like a second heartbeat that isn't mine.

When my eyes flutter open, I'm lying on a bed that looks carved from obsidian and starlight.

My clothes are gone. Not in a threatening way. Like they just went *poof.*

Or maybe replaced is a better word.

A silk sheet has been draped over me, fine and pale, like moonlight woven into fabric.

There he is. Standing at the foot of the bed.

Waiting for something. I don't know what.

Maybe he's waiting for me?

But no, that's ridiculous. I'm nothing, just a nobody, and he, *well*, he's certainly not nothing.

"You appear calm despite everything that's happened," Alaric says, voice dark with satisfaction.

Pride, maybe?

He lifts a hand, and with a casual flick of his fingers, a dress appears.

It unfurls mid-air. Black silk, soft and luminous, like it was pulled from the dreams of a fairytale queen.

He steps forward and lays it on the bed beside

me, his gaze trailing over my body with no shame, no hesitation.

Like he's memorizing me for some sacred purpose.

I pull the sheet tighter around myself, heart thudding.

"Wear this," he says, voice low and firm, holding out the same silk dress he conjured earlier—*out of thin air.*

It's not really a suggestion.

Not even close.

I get the distinct impression Alaric is used to being obeyed without hesitation.

Kings and CEOs have that tone.

Authoritative, absolute.

Only, I'm pretty sure this isn't a boardroom or a palace.

And also? I'm probably either dead or unconscious.

Because none of this feels real.

The glowing walls. The dress made of starlight. The man—*no, not a man*—who saved me from creeps in an alley and then somehow teleported me to this place that feels more dream than dimension.

So yeah. I'm definitely making this up.

A coma fantasy. Brain misfire. Final hallucination.

Before I can spiral, though, his voice slices through my panic.

"I assure you, you are very much alive, Jules Strano. Now," he says, giving the dress a little shake. "The dress?"

I blink. "You know my name?"

"I know a lot of things about you, *Myrrin*," he says, and it should sound arrogant, but somehow doesn't. "Now. Will you put it on?"

I hesitate. "Could I maybe get some privacy?"

He frowns like I just asked him to explain cryptocurrency. "Privacy?"

"I'm not exactly an exhibitionist," I mutter, tugging the blanket tighter around me. "I'm a big girl. Fat, okay? Not everyone's seven feet tall and built like a professional athlete, for Pete's sake."

His head tilts. Slowly. Like he's genuinely trying to solve a puzzle.

"You think you're big?"

"Yes," I say, defensive now. "I know I don't look like one of your ethereal elf women or whatever the standard is here in Nightfall, and I'm not trying to be all that. I just don't want to, I don't know. Make a scene or something."

He stares at me another beat, then says, perfectly serious, "I assure you, *Myrrin*, you look exactly how a female should. And as for big? I am enormous. You are exactly my scale."

I blink. "What?"

"You match me," he adds, voice quieter. "Perfectly."

Oh.

Oh no.

He turns, giving me his back with a quiet murmur. "If modesty calms you, I will not watch."

But I catch him in the mirror.

A flicker.

A slight narrowing of his dark brows.

His eyes, a strange mix of silver and obsidian, glowing faintly, tracking me through the reflection like he forgot mirrors exist.

And still, despite everything, in spite of the surreal setting and the intensity of him and the creeping certainty that I'm in way over my head—I do feel calm.

Just like he said I would.

I slip the dress over my head.

It glides down, weighing nothing at all.

Like air made into fabric.

Cool. Soft. Shocking in how perfectly it fits.

As if it were made for me.

And maybe it was.

He turns towards me once I stand, smoothing the impossibly smooth fabric over my hips, and his gaze drops to my body.

I want to suck in, but really, that wouldn't do much good in hiding the extra thirty or so pounds I carry around my middle.

So, I don't bother.

I'm thirty-two, far too old to still feel that same old insecurity.

But what can I say? I guess it's just a part of me.

Alaric straightens, then gestures to himself.

Broad shoulders. Towering height.

A presence that could surely blot out suns.

My mouth goes dry.

My heartbeat skips.

I've never seen anything like him.

"It is as I said. I am enormous," he says simply, as if stating a fact of nature. "And you, *Myrrin*, are perfectly sized for me."

My cheeks flush so hot they feel scorched.

He considers me for another beat, then nods once, turning his back again.

I sense his curiosity coiling just beneath the surface as I take a step. I wince at the cold hard stone and catch him watching once more in the mirror across the chamber.

Not with malice.

Not even simple lust.

It's more like hunger.

And fascination.

"Wait," he says, and before I can even ask what for, he's right there, suddenly kneeling at my feet.

The movement is so fluid, so unexpected, it steals the breath right out of my lungs.

One minute he's standing tall and untouchable, and the next, this massive, inhumanly beautiful male is lowering himself like I'm some kind of royalty.

Or something even more dangerous.

His hand hovers beneath my ankle, and I'm frozen, locked in his gaze.

Then he lifts one foot with surprising care and waves his hand over my skin.

A warm shimmer passes beneath his palm, like static wrapped in silk.

Boots appear.

But not just boots. These are *impossible.*

They mold perfectly to my feet—soft, support-ive, like some glorious union of buttery leather and memory foam.

They're heeled, which should be a crime, but somehow the three-inch wedge doesn't feel like punishment.

It feels like power. Balance.

I gasp, blinking down at them. "What—how did you—?"

"There," he murmurs, repeating the same conjuring motion with my other foot. "Now your feet will be protected, *Myrrin*."

That word again.

He's said it twice now.

I know he told me what it means, and really, it's innocent enough. But every time it leaves his lips, something inside me reacts.

Like it knows. Like it wants.

I feel like I've stepped inside a dream spun from someone else's memory.

But it's mine now.

Alaric rises in a single, elegant motion and offers me his hand.

"Come on," he says softly, "I want you to see."

I take his hand before I have time to overthink it. His palm is warm, strong, rough in all the right places.

He leads me to the far end of the chamber, where heavy curtains of deep indigo part at his command.

Beyond them is a glassless window, more of an arch, really, that opens to the world outside.

And, holy cow, what a world.

I step to the edge and stare.

Below, the landscape of Nightfall stretches out in eerie, breathtaking splendor.

Black grass ripples beneath a violet moon. Silver trees hum as wind moves through their branches—*not rustling, but singing.*

Rivers shimmer with upside-down reflections that ripple skyward instead of outward.

Winged beasts spiral across skies carved by stars that pulse like slow heartbeats.

It's beautiful.

Terrifying.

Alien.

Like looking into the soul of a place that remembers everything and forgives nothing.

I tear my eyes from it long enough to look at him.

He's watching me, his expression unreadable.

"So, what is all this?"

"I told you," Alaric says, his voice almost reverent as he steps beside me at the window. "This is Nightfall. A parallel realm. A place layered just beyond the human veil."

He pauses, watching me study the landscape like I'm trying to decide whether it's beautiful or terrifying.

"Here," he continues, "dreams are born. And nightmares are doled out with necessary care."

I turn to him slowly. "You're saying this is where dreams come from?"

"Yes," he murmurs, gaze distant. "Good and bad. The stories you wake from and can't quite remember? The ones that inspire paintings, books, music, even love? They begin here. Whispered from the mouths of Nightfall's winds. Spun into the minds of mortals while they sleep."

"And the nightmares?" I ask.

His smile is dark and quiet. "Also us. But not to torment. To warn. To shape. To keep your world, and others, from forgetting fear, or consequence. Nightmares are necessary, Jules. Without them, people would walk blindly into ruin."

The window glass shimmers faintly in response to his words—as if the realm itself agrees.

"You speak like this place is alive," I say softly.

He turns his eyes on me, and my breath catches.

"It is alive. It breathes. It listens. It chooses."

My heart thuds against my ribs.

"And it chose me?"

"I chose you," he says. "Not just the realm. The magic. The thread between us. You felt it, didn't you? In the alley. In the way your dreams shifted the moment you woke from your sleep safely ensconced in my bed."

I shake my head, overwhelmed. "But I'm just a bartender from New Jersey. I'm not magic. I'm not special."

"You are," he says, gently but without hesitation. "You're mine, *Myrrin*. And that makes you part of this realm now. Whether you believe in it yet or not."

I look at him, then back at the view.

Fields of dark grass.

A river glowing with upside-down stars.

Winged creatures curling through purple clouds like ink spilled into sky.

And somehow, impossibly, it feels like I've been here before.

Like I was always meant to arrive.

"But why am I really here, Alaric?" I whisper.

He doesn't flinch.

Doesn't evade.

Doesn't give me a speech full of prophecy or war.

He just says, simply, "You are here for me."

My breath catches. "What does that mean?"

"It means you are not alone anymore. You were always meant to be here."

His voice is low, rougher now. "In your deepest, darkest dreams you called out for someone to come to save you from loneliness and despair, *Myrrin*. I answered."

The wind catches my hair. The sky shifts. The stars seem to pulse faster.

And for some reason I can't explain, I don't cry or scream or run.

Not yet.

Nightfall.

It feels familiar.

I don't know how I know the name, but I do.

This place isn't Earth.

It isn't Hell.

It's somewhere in between.

And I have a feeling I've just become a thread in a story much older—*and far more dangerous*—than any I've ever owned.

CHAPTER 5
ALARIC

"I thought you might enjoy this," I say, gesturing toward the towering library chamber just beyond the arched door.

I watch her greedily as she steps over the threshold—*my threshold*—with wide eyes and parted lips.

While I'd been surveilling her in the human realm, I noticed the way she lingered in bookstores, the way she read late into the night on her small cellular device.

She sought escape in stories.

Longed for them.

And now I'm giving her an entire library.

"This is incredible," she breathes, her voice low,

reverent.

Her entire posture shifts, softens, like something inside her has uncoiled. She all but shimmers with quiet joy.

"Is this all yours?" she asks, eyes wide with genuine curiosity.

"The Eyrie is my legacy," I answer, standing a bit straighter. "And everything in it belongs to me."

I shouldn't care whether she's impressed.

But I do.

"Your house has a name?" she says with a grin, and something tightens in my chest.

I clear my throat. "Yes, most places here do."

She walks farther inside, trailing her fingers along the carved railings and weathered leather spines like she's touching something holy.

The way she looks at it all makes the air around her glow.

It's like she is maybe realizing for the first time that magic is real, and wonder isn't dead.

"In here, I have books from all corners of Nightfall," I tell her. "Histories. Mythologies. Grimoires. Adventures."

She pauses beside a shelf and grins again. "Any romance?"

The question catches me off guard, but I recover quickly.

"You won't need books for that, *Myrrin*," I murmur, meeting her gaze.

She bites her lower lip and looks away, but not before I see it.

The flush that spreads across her cheeks.

The way her breath stutters, just once.

The ripple of awareness that passes between us.

It's small. *But unmistakable.*

I find myself wondering at her reaction. I know it's genuine.

When was the last time someone blushed in my presence?

When was the last time I cared?

I admit, seduction isn't something I've had to practice.

As Alaric, *Demon Knight, Lord of Air, keeper of Winds, Guardian of Nightfall,* I have never lacked for admirers.

My name and titles carry power, prestige, allure.

But none of them—*none*—have ever stirred anything more than passing interest.

Until now.

Until her.

Jules Strano.

Human. Mortal. Inconveniently irresistible.

The thought alone has me frowning.

No. This isn't desire. This isn't fate.

She is a means to an end.

A vessel. A variable. The key to my ascension. A means to make me Prime.

That is all she is.

Then why do you have to keep reminding yourself?

I clasp my hands behind my back and follow her with careful detachment as she explores the room, still lit with wonder.

She brushes her fingers along a spine—*Nightfall's Golden Age*—and glances back at me, uncertain.

"Am I? That is, um, can I touch?" she asks, one brow arched, fingers resting lightly on the worn leather.

"Yes," I say, my voice lower than I intend.

And in truth, I wish she was asking to touch something else.

Someone else.

The thought angers me, too.

It's ridiculous for me to have these desires. Dangerous, too.

So I step back. Regroup. Reassert control.

"Touch whatever you like, but stay in here. I'll

return shortly," I tell her, turning toward the arch-way. "Before supper."

I glance back once.

She's already pulled a book from the shelf and is flipping through the pages with those delicate, fascinated hands—touching ancient knowledge like it's sacred. It's not reverence for power, not awe for magic. It's genuine wonder. And that, somehow, makes it worse.

"Try not to upset anything, *Myrrin*," I say dryly, the endearment once more slipping too easily from my tongue.

She snorts. "No promises."

I let the smile curl at my mouth, but only after I've turned away. She doesn't need to know how effortlessly she affects me. Not yet.

"Oh, Alaric?"

I stop mid-stride, one hand braced on the stone archway.

"Yes?"

She hesitates. "When can I go home?"

The words hit harder than they should.

My back stiffens. My jaw clenches.

Home?

She means Earth. Her little apartment. Her routine. Her sad little bar.

She doesn't understand yet that this—*Nightfall, me*—is where she belongs.

And the truth?

There's nothing for her to return to.

But saying never seems cruel.

Even if it's honest.

So I give her the answer I know she won't like, but that buys me time.

"We shall discuss that later. Now," I add, gesturing to the library, "stay in here."

"Sit, stay—what am I? A dog?" she snaps back.

I raise one brow in response. I don't have to say anything.

She huffs, crosses her arms. "Fine. Just tell me why."

And just like that, my already-thin patience frays.

I cross the distance between us in two long strides, crowding her against the nearest shelf, my body braced just a breath from hers.

She startles, eyes wide, lips parting, but she doesn't move away. Doesn't shrink.

Good.

She shouldn't.

She should know exactly who I am.

I tilt her chin upward with the pad of my thumb, forcing her gaze to meet mine.

Her skin is warm. Soft. Infuriatingly inviting.

"There are many things in Nightfall that can hurt a fragile human like you, *Myrrin*," I say, voice low and dangerous. "Because you are under my protection, any such act will be seen as an attack on me and my person. So, unless you want to provoke a war, you will stay here. Where it's safe. Until I come for you."

Her breath catches, but she holds my gaze. Proud. Defiant.

I like that too much.

"Now," I finish, "nod that you understand."

She rolls her eyes, muttering under her breath, "Can you be any more barbaric?"

But she nods.

And she's smiling.

Just a little. Just enough to make my control slip again.

I force myself to step back.

And she vanishes between the shelves, hips swaying slightly beneath that silk I conjured, unaware—*or perhaps entirely aware*—of the effect she has on me.

I watch her longer than I should.

Then, with one last lingering glance, I turn and leave her to the books.

And if I walk faster than usual down the hall toward the chamber where my brothers wait with the fate of Nightfall in a glass box, well, that's no one's business but mine.

The moment I step into the antechamber beyond the library's threshold, I feel them.

Not just their magic, but their moods.

Eager. Anxious. Angry.

Kael. Thorne. Dagan.

They're waiting for me beneath the vaulted ceiling of the outer hall, where moonlight bleeds in through the narrow glass teeth of the ceiling.

Ancient banners hang in silence overhead.

The weight of memory lingers here—*of oaths sworn, battles fought, crowns forged.*

Kael is the first to speak, lounging as if he belongs to the room.

"You found your human quickly," he says, eyes glinting with sea-glass amusement. "What did you do, whistle?"

"I followed the thread," I answer simply, but Dagan snorts and turns away, disgust curling his lip.

"You're going to trick a human into believing she's your fated mate?" he growls. "You'd bind an innocent soul to a lie, **enter a false** *zareth*, just to grab power?”

I raise a brow. “And you wouldn’t?”

“I’d rather die with honor than rule as a fraud.”

“Good,” I murmur. “Then we understand each other, Lord Dagan. Die and leave the throne to someone stronger.”

Before Dagan can lunge, Thorne chuckles from the shadows, stepping forward with fire flickering along the ends of his hair like it’s alive.

“So, this human. What is she like? What did it take to woo her to your side?”

“What do you care, Thorne? She is mine now,” I reply, wary of giving him, or really, any of them my back.

“Careful, Alaric,” he says, voice teasing, danger-ous. “You’re getting attached. What if I decide I want her instead?”

I go still.

The air drops ten degrees.

“If you try to take her,” I say softly, “I will put your fire out. Permanently.”

The threat lands. Thorne’s grin falters, then sharpens with challenge. But before he can reply, Kael raises a hand.

"Enough." His voice carries the weight of oceans, deep and unbothered.

"We didn't come to scratch at each other like feral beasts. We came for this."

He gestures, and with a ripple of magic, a box appears in the center of the room.

A glass cube, sealed with binding glyphs etched in molten silver.

Inside it rests the crown of Nightfall, taken from the head of our lost Prime.

Ancient. Glorious. Unclaimed.

It pulses faintly with dormant power, as if it knows what's at stake. As if it's waiting.

"We must guard it," Kael says, stepping forward. "The SoulTakers grow restless. Their scouts are sniffing along the outer planes. If they find it before a new Prime rises," he murmurs, leaving the rest unfinished.

We all know what will happen then. Kael doesn't need to tell us.

"They'll devour the realm," Dagan finishes grimly.

"So we bind it," Kael says. "With all our magic. And we leave it here, safe at Alaric's Eyrie. High above the shadows they cling to. The one place they're least likely to look."

I approach the box slowly.

The crown thrums in response, not quite recognition, but curiosity.

One by one, we raise our hands.

Each of us casts a ward, layering our power atop the last—*earth, sea, flame, and wind.*

Old magic. Sacred. Binding.

When the last symbol flares, Kael lets his hand fall and says quietly, "We all want it. But if we lose it, there won't be a realm left to rule."

For once, all three of us nod in agreement.

Even Thorne.

Even Dagan.

But as I glance back toward the library—*where Jules is surely still flipping through ancient texts with those delicate, ink-hungry fingers*—one thought crashes through me like a blade made of fire:

If they come for the crown, they'll come here.

And worse—*they'll come through her to get it.*

The SoulTakers won't just sniff at the edges of the Eyrie.

They'll scent the thread. The bond.

They'll sense her brightness, her humanity, her fragile power, and they'll twist it, corrupt it, use it against me.

The idea fills me with a feeling I haven't allowed myself in centuries.

Not just rage.

But fear.

And beneath that?

Pure, unadulterated wrath.

It rises from the pit of me, dark and vast.

My Dragon stirs.

He's been silent far too long, but now he rumbles, low and dangerous, beneath my skin.

Because he feels it too.

She is ours.

If they so much as touch her—*SoulTakers, rebels, even one of my own brothers*—destruction will follow.

Not strategy.

Not political precision.

No.

Destruction.

Plain and simple in its absolute devastation.

My hands tremble with the effort to contain it, my breath no longer smooth but shaking because the thought of losing her, of someone else laying claim to what is mine, ignites something primal in me.

The Dragon doesn't care about thrones or legacy or balance.

He cares about the soft creature now roaming my inner sanctum.

The one who blushes when I look at her.

The one who licks her lips and says my name like she doesn't yet understand the power she gives it.

I picture her again—*vivid as starlight*—those precious seconds when she stood bare, unaware she was being watched.

Her curves bathed in torchlight, the silk gown I conjured sliding over her hips like a kiss.

Fuck.

My cock thickens instantly, heavy and aching, and I press my palms flat against the cold stone wall of the Eyrie, grounding myself.

This isn't just attraction.

It's obsession.

Possession.

A mating bond.

The zareth?

I'm not sure.

But it is unwanted, unplanned, and unstoppable.

And it's happening faster than it should.

I might have misjudged the Dragon's connection to her.

Hell, I might've misjudged myself.

Because nothing—*nothing*—about Jules Strano has followed the plan.

Not her reaction to me.

Not her presence here.

Not the way she matters.

She's just a pawn.

But that doesn't feel right.

She's supposed to be a means to the throne.

But I think, well that is, I believe Jules Strano might actually be my *viyella*.

And after hearing Thorne's careless remark, I am positive I'll let no other have her.

Gods help anyone—*anyone*—who tries to take her from me.

I will burn Nightfall down to the bone before I let that happen.

CHAPTER 6
JULES

My thoughts are surprisingly clear.

I mean, yeah, I've been kidnapped.

Stolen.

Taken across some magical veil by a man with glowing eyes and a voice that could melt the spine out of a nun.

Captured, sure.

But weirdly?

Not exactly a hardship.

Because Alaric is tall, dark, and apocalyptically sexy in a way that should be illegal.

And when he looks at me like I'm something rare, something *his*, my whole body gets confused about what's happening.

Still, I should be panicking. Screaming. Plotting escape.

But here I am, calmly wandering through a *literal fantasy library*, running my fingers along books older than the United States, casually inhaling the scent of magic and dust like I belong here.

I *don't* belong here.

Do I?

I should want to go home.

But home to what?

My shitty apartment with the dripping faucet and the neighbor who blasts disco music at 3 a.m.?

To bartending for smug finance bros who tip like I'm a vending machine with boobs?

To overdue bills, aching loneliness, and a life that feels more like surviving than living?

Yeah. Hard pass.

So okay, go ahead.

Call me delusional.

Say I have Stockholm Syndrome.

That I'm the dumb girl in every B-horror flick who trips while running and gets snatched by the monster.

Whatever.

Because for the first time in *forever*, I feel alive.

Like I've stepped into a story I didn't even know I'd been aching for.

I'm not just watching life happen to someone else through a screen.

I'm *in* it.

Living it.

Breathing it.

Even if it feels unreal.

Even if this place is quiet. *Too quiet.*

Even if there's probably a talking book somewhere that's going to bite me.

And even if Alaric looks like the kind of dangerous, carved from granite warrior who could absolutely savage my body without breaking a sweat.

Yes, please.

Don't judge. It's been a while.

And Alaric? He looks like he knows how to *find* every single one of my secret places and then, make me beg for more.

Okay, don't look at me like that.

Blame the alien romance novels. Seriously, You read enough of these fantastic *taken-by-the-alpha-overlord-in-space* stories and your standards shift.

But the thing that really has me spiraling isn't what he could do to my body.

It's what he's already doing to my heart.

Because under the smirking, commanding, vaguely insufferable exterior, there's something else.

A grief.

A weight.

A *need*.

Like the only thing more dangerous than being near him is being gone from him.

That scares me more than his magic ever could.

Because bodies heal.

But hearts? Hearts get ruined.

And if I'm not careful, mine's going to *shatter* in the hands of a Demon who never meant to hold it.

"Wow," I whisper as I find what I've undoubtedly been searching for in this incredible museum of a library.

There's row upon row of shelves behind iron and glass doors.

"The *restricted section*," I murmur and grin to myself.

Okay, this part of the library gives silence new meaning.

I bite my lip, inching forward as I try to make out the shapes of the symbols or runes on some of the covers. These books are old. Like the ancient kinda *old*.

Mystical.

And the quiet that seems to shroud this area?

It's the kind of quiet that only exists in churches or the woods just before something happens in a horror movie.

I squint and try to make out some of the words, but to do that I need to step closer.

Something pulses in the air.

"*Shifting Realms*," I whisper, proud of myself for making that one out.

"*The Ritual of the Zareth: Forging Soul Bonds in Nightfall*," I pause, wondering what that even means.

Then, I move on to the next title.

This enormous book is on a shelf by itself. There's a glow inside, like the book emanates light, and I have to stand on my tippy toes to even try to make out the words.

The cover seems to be made of pure silver and gold. Etched into the metal is a crown, like the kind you'd see in some fantasy flick directed by Peter Jackson.

"*The R-Rise of the,*" I whisper, and try to get higher.

I look around, see a small box, and I grab it, placing it in front of the shelf.

I step up and try again, my heart in my throat as I finally see the full title.

"*The Rise of the Prime of Nightfall.*"

I touch my hand to the glass, I just can't seem to help it, and the book?

I swear to God, it's like the book *exhales*.

"Shit," I mumble, stepping back and literally falling on my ass.

I peek around, but no one sees me. So, I dust myself off and leave that aisle.

Restricted sections aren't for me.

I wander deeper into the stacks.

The air changes the farther I go—*thicker, quieter, like even the books are holding their breath.*

I trail my fingers over the rows of leather-bound volumes, some of them glowing faintly, others humming beneath my touch like they know I'm here.

And I mean, come on.

This is every book girl's dream, right?

That *Beauty and the Beast* fantasy, where the brooding, misunderstood monster gifts you a library so big you could live in it and never finish reading.

Only, let's be real.

I'm no Beauty. Not with my curves and my sarcasm and my habit of trusting absolutely no one.

And Alaric? He might be a Demon Lord, or some dark god of kidnapping chunky humans, but he isn't my Beast.

He's something else entirely.

Something more dangerous.

Because the Beast had rules. Boundaries.

Alaric has intentions—ones I can't read, and ones I'm starting to feel in places I probably shouldn't.

Still, I can't stop the part of me that's secretly, silently thrilled.

Because, this place?

This world?

The impossible, beautiful, terrifying Nightfall?

It feels more like home than anything ever has.

CHAPTER 7

JULES

"Oh, you're not in Kansas anymore," I murmur as I stop in front of an enormous statue at the end of one aisle.

It's a man, or *something*. I mean, it looks familiar, but not.

The statue is just breathtaking, commanding of all my attention. So damn majestic, I feel tears pricking my eyes.

He has horns and wings and so many muscles, I feel kind of pervy, gaping at it the way I am.

"I wonder who you are," I whisper, then continue on my journey.

The scent here is strange but pleasant—old

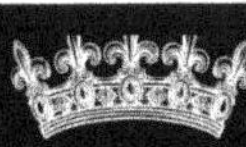

parchment and polished stone, with something faintly floral, like the ghost of lavender.

The deeper I go, the less the air feels like it belongs to me.

It gets heavier. Denser.

And the little warning bells I was just starting to believe didn't work anymore start ringing inside my head.

That's when I see her.

A woman—tall and thin, graceful, with luminous bronze skin and crimson hair that spills down her back like wildfire.

She stands on a ladder, shelving books like she's done it a thousand times, humming something soft and eerie under her breath.

Her eyes flick toward me.

Black. Fully, entirely black.

Like ash, like onyx.

I freeze.

She frowns. Worried, maybe? Or just surprised?

I'm not sure. But I'm tired of talking to myself, so I go for it.

"Hello," she says, her voice like cool water poured over hot metal. Soothing, but startling.

"You must be the hoo-man Lord Alaric brought here."

"Um, I guess," I say, blinking at the elegant figure high on the ladder. "And you are?"

She slides down the last few rungs and lands without a sound, bowing slightly with one hand over her chest.

"My name is *Shade*, mistress. One of the Eyrie's stewards."

Her name fits.

There's something smoky about her. Not dark, not threatening. More like dusk in motion.

Her skin is luminous gray, eyes like polished ash, and her hair spills in a sheet of crimson fire down her back. She moves like she could vanish between shadows without a trace.

I stare. My heart's thudding harder than it should be, and not because I'm afraid.

"Forgive me for asking, but *what* are you?"

She smiles. Just a small tilt of the lips, not entirely warm, not entirely cruel.

"A Demon, of course. Nightfall's premier population comprises Demons."

Of course. Like that's just a thing now.

She tilts her head, studying me with those ink-black eyes.

"And you're a hoo-man, yes? Here to be our Lord's *viyella*?"

"It's human," I correct gently. "And you can call me Jules." Then I blink. "Wait—what was that you just said? Your Lord's *what*?"

"Pardon, mistress, um, Lady Jules?" she tries, awkward now.

"Just Jules," I say again.

But she looks uncertain, like calling me anything less than nobility might get her smote by a lightning bolt. So I let it go.

"Anyway, you said I'm Lord Alaric's *what*?"

"Oh, um..." She shifts like she's suddenly realized she's said too much. "I don't think it is for me to explain, Lady—I mean, Just Jules."

There's a soft humming sound at the back of her throat, something melodic and strange, and it somehow calms me.

Like the magic in her voice is designed to soothe skittish humans.

She turns to resume stacking books on the rolling cart behind her.

"I will continue with my duties, if you please."

"Wait," I say, reaching out and touching her arm without thinking.

She goes completely still.

I quickly pull back, realizing I've broken some unspoken rule.

"Sorry. I didn't mean to offend. I just," I murmur and exhale. "Can we talk? Just for a bit?"

She looks down at where I touched her, then up again with something almost like surprise. Then she gives a small nod.

"Sure, Just Jules. We can talk," she says carefully. "If I may work while we do? There is much to be done."

"Of course! I can even help," I offer, eager for connection.

Something normal.

Even if it's between a human and a gray-skinned Demon steward with a lullaby for a voice.

Shade shakes her head with a ghost of amusement, but doesn't shoo me away.

I take that as a win.

"I suppose it is confusing," she murmurs, gently shelving another book. "Being in a new realm."

"That's one word for it," I say. "Another is terrifying. A third might be shocked by all the beauty here. I mean, are all Demons hot-as-hell, so to speak?"

Shit. Did I just stick my foot in my mouth?

I wait for her anger, but instead, Shade simply hums again. And this time I swear it's almost a laugh.

"You mean you find our Lord attractive?"

I shrug, lips twitching. "I mean, you are only the second person, er, Demon, I've ever met, and you are stunning."

"Thank you," she says, eyes wide. "And Lord Alaric? You find him stunning also?"

"Oh, well, he's not *not* hot."

"The temperature is quite cool," she frowns.

"Oh, yeah, I know. I mean hot as in like sexy, attractive," I explain, blushing.

"I see. Well, he is *famed* among the servants," she says diplomatically. "Though no one has ever seen him quite like this before."

"Like what?"

Her eyes flick to mine, unreadable.

"Determined."

A shiver trails down my spine.

"So, um, how long have you worked here? Is Alaric a good boss? My old boss sucked," I mutter.

"Boss? Lord Alaric is fair and just. I've been in his employ since I've come of age," she explains.

"I see," I reply, but of course, I am lying. Still, I don't want to give up my new friend, so I walk while she shelves books, and I ask questions.

"Your duties? What are they?"

"Well, I tend the library. And sometimes I work in the kitchen. I also have sentry duties."

"Sentry duties? Like in the army?" I am clearly confused.

"All the Eyrie's attendants are trained in the art of war," she replies.

"Wow. How often do you have to fight?"

"Whenever it is needed," she replies and shivers race down my spine.

"So, um, this room is huge. I've been in here for at least an hour and I can't find the end of it."

I change the subject. Because, war? I don't know anything about it.

"The library stretches for miles," Shade replies, and turns down one particular aisle, seeming to pull a cart with books out of thin air.

I follow her without quite meaning to.

There's something mesmerizing about the way she moves so elegantly.

Like silk caught on a breeze.

"How did you do that?" I ask cautiously.

"Do what, mistress? Oh, the cart? It is stored in a *holding space,* a vacuum if you will," she says. "I can reach through the veil with my magic and retrieve what is needed in order to return it."

"Wow, I've never seen magic," I confess, staring as she does it again, slowly.

"Magic is very much a part of the fabric of Nightfall."

"We don't have that on Earth," I begin, but she shakes her head.

"Magic is everywhere. There would be nothing without it. But I understand it is harder to see in some realms."

I swallow, processing what she said and have to agree. She is probably right.

I watch her work in silence for a few more minutes.

"So, is everyone here as, um, friendly as you?"

Shade's laugh is bright and sharp.

"Oh no, Just Jules, you must be wary. Nightfall is fraught with terrors."

Well. That's comforting. Not.

She continues, unfazed.

"The SoulTakers have been closing in. Nasty things. They feed on dreams, you know. Slip into your mind while you sleep and peel the edges of your soul away, one layer at a time."

I nearly trip. "I—what?"

"Oh yes," she says lightly, as if discussing the weather. "They're why Great Lords like Alaric and his brethren exist. They keep the balance. Protect what's left of the realm."

She pauses, running a fingertip along the spine of a book bound in what looks suspiciously like scales.

"But with the fall of the Prime," her voice fades. Then Shade's tone darkens. "Well, I'm afraid things have grown unstable."

I take that in.

A realm ruled by elemental Demon Lords.

A magical crown.

Dream-eating monsters.

And me.

A bartender from Jersey.

"So, what am I doing here? If he is so busy with all of this, why did he take me?" I ask before I can stop myself.

Shade stops walking.

Turns to me.

Her eyes soften. Not with pity, but something else. Maybe respect?

"That's a question only Lord Alaric can answer," she says. "But if the realm allowed you to pass through, then I'd say *you belong here*. Nightfall does not grant everyone that right. If it let you in, then there is more to you than you think, Just Jules."

I bite the inside of my cheek, suddenly over-whelmed.

This place isn't just some dream I'm going to wake up from. It's real. Magical. Terrifying.

And somehow, I'm a part of it.

But *how long* can I stay?

And what will it cost me if I do?

CHAPTER 8
ALARIC

The Eyrie—Approaching the Library

My brothers leave after we finish putting wards around the crown.

But I remained standing there long after they'd gone, with Kael's parting words haunting me.

"Maybe this idea of yours, that humans are soft and easy to fool, that you could trap one with your magic and charm, isn't exactly what you thought, my old friend. Maybe it's she who's trapped you?"

Fucking Kael. Lord of asinine comments.

I growl my frustration.

I need to refocus. This isn't about her. It never was.

It's about the crown.

About the realm.

About doing what none of my brothers have managed so far—*claiming the Prime seat before the SoulTakers breach the veil and reduce everything we've protected to dust.*

Jules is a piece in that puzzle.

Nothing more.

So why the fuck do I keep thinking about her mouth?

Her lips parted when I lifted her chin.

The heat in her eyes when she asked me why I brought her here.

The way her body reacted before her mind caught up.

Curious, open, wanting.

I grind my teeth as I stride down the corridor, every torch I pass flaring slightly at my presence.

My magic is restless, coiling under my skin like a storm in waiting.

It's time to turn up the heat.

Time to shift from restraint to charm.

Seduction.

I'm good at it.

I've made gods beg and monsters purr. Mortals are *simple.*

One taste. One touch. And they bend.

Beneath the glamour I cast so I appear more

human to her—*palatable, familiar, safe*—I can feel the truth of me stir.

My wings stretch in the space between realms, aching to unfurl.

My Dragon's scales rustle beneath my skin like armor ready for war.

I don't like this game of pretending.

My Dragon doesn't understand the need for this *softness*.

It is simply illusion.

All of it.

The neat, symmetrical face.

The smooth, tamed magic that hums along the edges of my body like a well-mannered breeze.

But then again—*what isn't an illusion?*

How many centuries have I worn masks and played at civility?

For the comfort of mortals.

For politics.

For power.

This is no different.

And yet *it is*.

Because she's different.

I glance at Jules where she stands beneath the golden light of the library's dome, her fingers curled around the edge of a leather-bound tome, her cheeks flushed from some half-teasing remark she made a moment ago.

She radiates warmth, life, and maddening curiosity.

She turns and sees me, like she senses my approach. And I have to wonder at that.

Now she's looking at me like I'm something tame.

Like I'm just a man.

And for some reason I can't explain, that makes something twist inside me.

How would she react if I showed her my true form?

If she saw the curling horns that rise from my temples, carved with ancient markings older than her world?

The runes and rituals inked into my skin—sigils of air, war, and vengeance?

If my black wings burst forth, stretching wide and terrible, each feather tipped with obsidian?

If my hands morphed into what they really are— claws, not fingers, built for rending rather than caressing?

Would she scream?

Would she run?

Would she look at me with fear instead of

curiosity?

Would she call me *monster*?

And suddenly, I care.

My frown deepens, unbidden. A crack in the composure I've spent a lifetime perfecting.

I'm not supposed to care what a mortal thinks of me.

I'm not supposed to crave the way she looks at me now.

Like she wants to understand, not just survive.

I tell myself this is still a game. A strategy.

I tell myself that once I've completed the mating bond and claimed the crown, the feelings will fade.

But the lie tastes bitter in my mouth.

And my Dragon—*ancient, primal, unchainable*—rumbles low with a single, insistent truth.

She is mine.

My viyella.

And I want her to know all of me.

I want her to choose me.

No. I must stop this.

I will not let myself get sentimental.

That way lies weakness. Attachment.

And I have no time for either.

I will woo her, mate her, and claim the crown.

Then she'll be cared for.

Kept. Adored, if she wishes.

But nothing more.

Nothing *emotional.*

My steps slow as I approach.

Her scent reaches me now—warm cream and shea butter with a hint of human anxiety and something wilder beneath.

Something that stirs the Dragon inside me.

When I step farther inside, I find she is not alone.

She's standing beside Shade, one of my most loyal stewards.

The Demon is carefully shelving a row of fragile glass-bound volumes, but her attention is split.

Clearly she is fascinated by the mortal chattering beside her.

Jules is smiling.

Relaxed.

Her arms folded beneath her full breasts as she tilts her head, asking questions.

I catch her laugh, light and unsure, and something inside me sharpens.

I do not like that she is this at ease with anyone but me.

Mine.

The word carves itself into my bones.

Shade catches my gaze and immediately straightens, bowing her head. "My Lord."

Jules turns, and I see her face light up with something between curiosity and—*gods help me*—fondness.

Dangerous.

Too fucking dangerous.

I should end this now.

Shut her down.

Remind her what I am.

But instead—I watch.

Because Jules Strano, little mortal firebrand, has no idea the line she's toying with, and yet, she dances on it like she was born for this.

"Am I interrupting?" I ask, voice silken with that lazy authority mortals usually trip over themselves to obey.

She turns, one hand on her hip, chin tipped up in challenge.

"Depends," she says with a smirk. "You here to whisk me away to another realm—oops, wait. You did that already."

A joke?

She's joking.

With me.

Shade gasps softly at her audacity. Even lowers her gaze, which amuses me more.

Because normally? That kind of insolence would earn a lesser creature a quick, painful lesson in fear.

But this isn't just anyone.

This is her.

Jules doesn't stop. Of course not.

"Or," she continues, tilting her head with mock curiosity, "are you going to give me more cryptic answers about why you've brought me here? You know—because being *chosen* really doesn't explain the kidnapping part."

Audacious. Clever. Nervy.

She should be groveling. Trembling.

Instead, she's playing with me like she's in control.

I find myself amused.

So I don't interrupt. I wait. Let her finish.

And Jules?

She does not disappoint.

Her eyes sparkle, lips curling as she adds, "Or—*Heaven forbid*—is big bad Lord Alaric finally ready to answer some real questions?"

Shade makes a strangled sound like she's trying to disappear into the book cart beside her.

And me?

I smile.

Slowly.

Oh yes.

Time to turn it on.

I stalk forward, not too fast, not threatening—just enough for the air to thicken between us, enough for her breath to hitch even as she holds her ground.

"No more riddles," I murmur, letting the timbre of my voice darken just slightly. "I've kept you waiting long enough."

Jules's lashes flutter. Just once.

Good.

"You want answers?" I ask, stopping just short of touching her. My power hums in the space between us like heat lightning. "Then you may ask your questions over dinner. But I warn you, *Myrrin*, truth in Nightfall always comes with a price."

Her throat works as she swallows, but her gaze doesn't drop. Not yet.

And gods help me, I hope it never does.

I step closer, gaze raking down her silk-clad form, letting my power warm the space between us.

"Of course, I was thinking, if you're brave enough, that perhaps we might move beyond questions."

She blinks. "What's that supposed to mean?"

I let my gaze linger. Let the tension build. "It means I've been patient. But there are *other ways* to show you why you're here, *Myrrin*."

Her breath catches.

Good.

Because I'm done pretending I don't want her.

And if charm won't do the job, seduction will.

However, no one said I have to rush.

The hunt is more satisfying when the prey doesn't know it's already caught.

I let my fingers trail down her bare arm. Light enough to make her shiver, deliberate enough to make her wonder.

Jules stills, her breath catching ever so slightly.

Yes. She feels it.

I lift her hand, slow and certain, and guide it to the crook of my elbow. My other arm hovers behind her back, not touching, but close enough to claim.

"Hungry?" I ask, voice low.

Her eyes flick up, confused. "What?"

I lean in, close enough that my breath grazes the shell of her ear.

"Are you hungry, *Myrrin*?" I enunciate each syllable, letting her feel every word the way a body feels heat before it burns.

She doesn't answer. Not with her mouth.

But her body, *oh*, her body speaks volumes.

The soft rise of her chest. The flush blooming across her collarbone.

The way her fingers twitch against my arm, tightening just a little, as if testing the tension between us.

I glance down at her, at the woman I've stolen from one world and dragged into mine.

She's wrapped in silk, curves lush and inviting, eyes wide with disbelief and something she hasn't named yet.

But I know it.

Want. Desire. Yearning.

Even if she doesn't.

Not yet.

"Come, *Myrrin*," I murmur, pulling her gently forward. "Let me feed you."

Her gaze holds mine for one breathless second too long.

And then, slowly, she nods.

One step. Then another.

And I smile.

Because she doesn't know it yet, but with every step she takes at my side, she steps deeper into me.

I've got you now, Jules Strano.

CHAPTER 9
JULES

THE EYRIE—DINING HALL

The dining room in the Eyrie is like something out of a fever dream.

Polished black stone gleams beneath my booted feet. But I can still feel it somehow.

Warm and smooth, despite looking like it should be cold.

The walls are draped in massive woven tapestries—*some dark and violent, others bright with gold thread*—and the weirdest thing is, they move.

I blink at one, and I swear the characters inside shift slightly.

A warrior lifts his sword.

A woman turns her head and mouths something soundless.

"Are they alive?" I whisper.

Alaric glances at the tapestries.

"They are enchanted. They show pieces of our history. Each time you look, you might see something new."

Okay. No big deal.

"Like living history blankets. Okay," I murmur.

Totally normal.

He quirks an eyebrow at me, then we step farther into the room, and the scent of whatever's on the table wraps around me like some decadent cloud of temptation.

My stomach growls. Loudly.

The table itself stretches long and wide, carved from dark wood that looks older than most countries.

And it's already filled with food. Plates and platters are piled high with things I don't even recognize, but they smell amazing.

No servants. No awkward hovering.

Just the two of us.

Thank goodness, because I'd already feel weird enough being waited on in this dress.

Yes, this dress.

The silk one Alaric conjured for me.

The one that clings in the right places and glides everywhere else.

I probably shouldn't love it as much as I do. But I do.

Especially now that I see him.

Because holy hell.

He's wearing tight black pants and one of those flowy shirts you only see in period dramas or fantasy movies.

Like if a pirate and a fae king had a lovechild and then trained him in seduction.

"How do you always look like you're ready to ruin someone's life at a royal ball?" I mutter, eyes shamelessly sweeping him.

His smirk is slow and devastating.

"Yours, in particular, would be my preference."

My mouth goes dry.

"Careful, Lord Alaric. You'll make a girl feel special."

"Good. Because you are special, *Myrrin*."

His voice wraps around my name like silk and smoke.

We sit.

Or I try to sit gracefully, which is hard when my legs still feel jelly-like from how he looks at me.

He serves me first—*yes, actually serves me*—

scooping something sweet and savory onto my plate before tending to his own.

The food? Ridiculous.

Like magic met comfort food and decided to flex.

Tender meats with flavors I can't name but want to chase.

Fruit that bursts like sunlight on my tongue.

Bread so soft it could make angels weep.

And the whole time, he watches me.

As if each bite I take is something he's hoarded. Something that feeds him, too.

We talk.

Well, sort of.

It's a mix of banter and flirtation, little challenges and teases.

He tells me about Nightfall's skies and this special stone that if you hold it, it will change color when you lie.

I tell him he talks like a walking storybook.

At one point, he reaches over and brushes a crumb from my lip, and I swear my entire soul short circuits.

Then, when I've eaten more than I should admit, he sits back, wineglass in hand, and lets his eyes rake slowly down my body.

"Well," he murmurs, voice darkening with intent, "I believe it's time for dessert."

"Oh? And what's on the menu?" I tease, even though my pulse stutters.

His smile is dangerous now. Lethal in that beautiful, slow way.

"You are."

"Why me?" I ask, because really, *why me?*

I can't fathom a single reason why someone like him would choose to take me—*a chubby bartender from Jersey*—to this magical place.

"Because in all my travels, Jules Strano, in all the centuries I have walked this realm, I cannot imagine a single being I would rather have here with me right now."

And before I can come up with a single witty response, Alaric moves, crossing the distance between us in the blink of an eye.

His face hovers for a moment. His pupils elongate. Like something else is watching me from within him, then he moves.

He kisses me.

Not gently. Not hesitantly.

Like he's claiming something.

Like he knows this kiss will taste better than anything in this world or the next.

And fuck me, he's right.

Because when his mouth captures mine, when his hands slide to my waist and he lifts me from my chair, dragging me closer to his impossibly hard body, *everything else disappears.*

CHAPTER 10
ALARIC

"Alaric," she breathes against my lips, and fuck, my name has never sounded like that.

Like prayer and sin at once.

She clings to me like I'm something good.

Something worthy.

But I'm not any of that.

I am lies.

I am illusion.

This is seduction. Practiced and planned.

"Will you give yourself to me, Jules Strano?" I ask, my voice rougher now.

"I've never felt like this before. It's crazy. You're like a dream. A stranger in the night whisking me away to some faraway fairytale," she whispers, and

her eyes—*fuck*, they look at me with so much heat I can't resist it.

I kiss her again.

"I asked you something," I remind her, wanting to kick myself and needing her answer all at the same time.

"You asked if you can have me," she says.

But this time, she makes the first move, pulling my head down so she can claim my lips with hers.

"And?" I whisper, holding on by a thread.

This woman lights fires in my blood.

She has no idea of the beast that lurks beneath my skin.

No notion of the monster she's teasing with promises of carnal delights and *ownership*.

Fuck, yes.

My Dragon likes that idea. He wants to own her, *to possess her*.

If I was the confessing kind, I'd admit I want that, too.

I can't wait to sink into her lush body, fill her with my seed, my scent.

To claim her with my bite.

My viyella.

She grins, stepping back. Cool air slips between us, and I hate it.

"And this is me **saying yes**," she says, reaching for the hem of her gown.

I don't wait. I can't.

So, I pounce. I drag her temptingly plump body to mine.

So damn soft.

"Tell me why first?" I ask, and yes, I still want to kick myself.

What am I doing giving her an out?

Asking questions when I should be claiming her?

"Because I trust you," she says, and that damn near breaks me.

"I'm not safe, *Myrrin*. Not even close."

Her reply? A soft, wicked little kiss and a whispered, "I didn't say you were safe. I said I trust you."

A pause. A flutter.

"So, what are you going to do with me now that I said yes?"

Her voice is a caress.

A challenge.

My chest tightens like a fist around glass, because she doesn't know what she's just done.

What it means to trust someone like me.

A Demon.

A liar.

A Lord of Illusion and hunger and too many secrets.

But gods help me, I'm going to take everything she's offering.

And then some.

I drag her back to me, one hand slipping around her waist while the other fists in her hair, angling her mouth so I can claim it again. The way I want to.

Roughly, deeply this time.

Our kiss ignites like dry lightning across a velvet sky.

Her dress is gone with a flick of my fingers, magic shredding silk like water against rock.

She gasps as I lift her easily, *possessively*, cradling her thighs around my hips as I walk us to the bed.

"*Myrrin*," I murmur, reverent and ravenous, "I'm going to worship every inch of you."

She laughs softly, breath catching as her back meets the bed.

"You talk like the villain in my very own fantasy novel starring me."

"I am the villain in your fantasy novel," I admit as I crawl over her, stripping away my own clothes, my horns gleaming in the firelight now that illusion has been fully discarded.

"But even villains can bring pleasure."

"You don't look like a villain," she whispers.

And as if of its own accord the rest of my illusion shatters.

Her eyes widen as she takes in the full truth of me.

Wings spanning almost the entire room, runes etched into my skin, claws extending from my fingers, fangs protruding from my gums, and silver fire dancing in my eyes.

But Jules? She doesn't flinch.

She reaches.

Touches.

Claims.

And my soul sings.

The moment her palm lays over the mark glowing just beneath my collarbone, something ancient stirs between us.

An echo of the zareth already whispering through the ether.

I can hardly breathe for the magic swirling around us. It's like I'm mesmerized by her. Bewitched.

Maybe she isn't mortal? Maybe I made a mistake thinking her human?

Jules Strano is more dangerous than she appears.

Still, I lower my mouth to hers, driving my tongue inside, claiming her with this kiss.

Then I travel lower, dropping biting kisses on her neck, her magnificent breasts—*tip-tilted and topped with dusky nipples I want to devour*—but I'm not finished exploring.

So, I continue licking and nibbling her soft skin to her stomach, her thighs, the soft curls covering her mound, trailing fire with every breath.

Her moans are magic, casting spells on me to keep me there, gifting her pleasure.

Her trembling, a vow, an oath to never stop until she screams my name.

And when I finally slide my fingers between her silky, wet folds, it's like an act of devotion.

"There you are, *Myrrin*," I murmur before I lick into her hot, glistening pussy.

She tastes—fuck, she tastes like mine.

Spicy and tangy, her sweet musk balancing it all and it's like ambrosia.

She moans and mewls, arching off the bed, but I'll have none of that. I'm in charge here. And I let her know by sucking on her clit and holding her down gently.

"Alaric," she whimpers, clutching at my hair while her orgasm crests over her.

I crave her passion, so I keep going. Licking her into her next climax, but by then, fuck me, this sassy little human has her hands wrapped around my horns.

My fucking horns.

My cock hardens even more and precum leaks from the tip. I almost can't take it, so I back off to tell her.

"Not the horns," I growl, lifting my head.

"Why? Does it hurt?" she asks, lifting up on her elbows and watching me with pupils blown.

"No, *Myrrin*. It doesn't hurt. But I want to be inside of you when I come."

"Oh fuck, that's hot. I want that, too. Please," she murmurs, licking her lips and reaching for me.

I wasn't planning on this.

Not tonight.

But with Jules beneath me, writhing, offering, waiting, I lose the last thread of restraint.

The room is bathed in moonlight, soft and blue as magic itself. It spills across the bed, gilding her bare skin in silver.

Her body—*gods*—her body is fucking glorious.

Full. Plush. Warm. Real.

She's spread across my sheets like she was always meant to be here.

Hair wild. Lips parted. Cheeks flushed.

Her curves rise and fall with each breath, and the sight of her like this?

Waiting for me, wanting me?

It makes my cock throb painfully.

I can't breathe. I don't want to.

I rise to my knees, nudging her legs open with mine, and place myself at her slick entrance.

She's already dripping for me—*soft, wet heat beckoning like a siren.*

I grip her hips, steadying her, steadying myself.

"This is when I claim you, *Myrrin*," I growl, voice rasping through the quiet. "This is when I make you mine."

And then I push in.

Fuck.

Tight. Hot. Perfect.

My eyes slam shut at the first squeeze of her around me, and my control shatters into ash.

I slide in deeper, inch by aching inch, until I'm buried to the hilt inside the most exquisite fucking heat I've ever known.

She moans. Her head is thrown back, lips forming my name like a curse and a promise.

"Alaric," she gasps.

I pull out slowly, just to the tip, then slam back

in, hard enough to make the headboard crack against the stone.

She is tight. Small. And I know I'm well-endowed. I should go slow.

But I can't. Something won't let me.

I need to savage her. To make her mine in every way.

But I know she feels pleasure.

I can sense it.

Fuck, I can still taste it.

Her legs wrap around me, heels pressing into the small of my back, and I give in to the rhythm.

Hard. Deep.

Slow. Then fast.

Fucking her like I need her to live.

Because honestly? I think I do.

The sound of our bodies slapping together echoes in the chamber, matched only by her moans and my gritted curses.

She feels too good. Too right.

Her nails drag down my back, then up again. Her eyes are locked on mine as she does it—slides her nimble fingers up my neck, caressing my face, and then my horns.

Fuck. Me.

I roar.

Pleasure jolts up my spine, touching every nerve ending.

She's everywhere, everything.

My wings snap open behind me, shadows stretching across the walls.

The runes carved into my flesh burn like fire, glowing brighter with each thrust.

Magic pulses from my skin to hers, the air sparking with every grind of her hips against mine.

We are wild together.

Desperate. Ruined.

She's close. I feel it.

"Let go for me," I whisper into her neck, licking the skin where I'll soon leave my mark. "Come, Jules."

And gods, she does.

Her pussy clenches so tight I nearly explode.

She cries out, shattering under me, her back arching, body spasming, voice breaking.

I follow with a savage growl, thrusting hard one last time, emptying myself deep inside her as my fangs pierce her shoulder.

I bite.

I claim.

And that's when the world detonates.

Magic erupts from our joined bodies—silver lightning crashing through the air, blinding and hot.

The bed shakes.

The walls quake.

My wings flare wide, catching the blast of raw power as a bond forms between us.

Unbreakable. Irrefutable.

Real.

I see it, my mark as it sears into her skin in glowing silver.

An ancient symbol.

A tether.

A soul-knot.

This is it. The Zareth.

It shouldn't be possible. Not with a human. Not like this.

But I feel it.

Like a silver tether locked around our hearts and anchored deep into Nightfall's core.

And suddenly, all my plans—*my schemes, my lies, my illusions*—mean nothing.

Because this bond doesn't lie.

This magic does not bend.

And it scares the shit out of me.

I look down at her. She's panting, glowing, marked with my bite and filled with my seed.

Her eyes—*half-lidded and dazed*—find mine.

"Wow. W-what was that?" she breathes.

I press my lips to her temple and whisper the only truth that matters now:

"It means you are mine, *Myrrin*. My *viyella*."

Impossible.

And yet *real*.

Her body shivers beneath mine, a tremor of aftershocks rippling through her as her hand lifts to the place where I bit her.

My mark glows faintly, silver and fire beneath her skin.

Claimed. Bound. Mine.

She touches it gently, fingers brushing the bruised flesh, and lifts those dark eyes to mine.

"And are you mine, Alaric?" she asks, teasing, playful—yet there's something raw in her voice.

Something unguarded.

She doesn't know what that question does to me.

The words are light on her lips, but they strike with deadly precision.

Because yes—*gods help me*—yes, she's nailed it.

The bond isn't one-sided.

It was never meant to be.

I lower my head and kiss her neck, lips brushing

the heat of the mark, the pulse of magic still throbbing between us.

She tastes like wild air and the promise of ruin.

I breathe her in and try to lie.

But I can't.

Not to her.

Not anymore.

My voice breaks the silence. It's rough, low, barely above a whisper.

"I might just be yours."

And the second I say it, I know the truth I've been dodging has finally caught up to me.

Because I don't just want her anymore.

I need her.

Not as a pawn.

Not as part of a plan.

But as the one thing I never thought I'd have.

A home.

And that terrifies me more than the SoulTakers ever could.

CHAPTER II
JULES

THE EYRIE—THE BEDROOM

I wake up alone.

The deep midnight-colored sheets are tangled around my feet, but I'm not cold.

Nope. I'm still warm. Still humming in all the right places.

My body is deliciously sore, like I've just danced through a storm and survived with fire in my veins and kisses pressed into my skin like secret spells.

Alaric.

The Demon Lord.

The one who wrecked me.

The one who stole me away from everything I knew.

And even crazier? He makes me want to stay.

It feels silly, maybe even dangerous, but—*gods*—I miss him.

Is that insane?

I mean, sure, the whole *abducted by a seven-foot-tall fantasy man with wings* situation might raise a few red flags.

Wings? Can you believe it?

And horns.

My face burns as I remember the way he came apart when I stroked his horns.

Who knew that was a Demon's sexy place?

I bite my lip and sigh.

Any good book girl will tell you that last night? That was the stuff of fantasy.

That was the moment the heroine falls hard and fast, and suddenly, the world tilted on its axis and everything—*I mean, everything*—starts to make sense.

And yeah, I know what you're thinking.

I shouldn't be so complacent. I shouldn't be swooning.

But no one—*no one*—has ever made me feel the way Alaric does.

Like I'm more than a body.

More than a nuisance.

Like I matter.

Growing up, I was never anyone's priority.

My parents were always too busy with each other, their problems, their affairs, their wine glasses.

I was the afterthought.

The responsibility neither of them asked for.

The one who made her own lunches, who walked herself to school in too-small shoes and came home to an empty house.

No bedtime stories. No hugs. No warmth.

So yeah, maybe that's why I'm clinging so hard to this impossible thing now.

To this dark-eyed, too-handsome man who looks at me like I'm the fucking magic even though he's the one who's magical.

This is my chance—*maybe my only chance*—to believe in something more.

To live the dream I only ever thought I'd read about.

And heck no, I'm not going to let it slip through my fingers just because it feels too good to be true.

I grin like a lunatic and sit up, grabbing the sheet to clutch it around my chest, when I hear soft footsteps outside the door.

"Alaric—?" I call, hopeful.

But it's not him.

"Good morning, Lady Jules," Shade greets me with her usual melodic voice, stepping into the room like she belongs in a painting.

My grin softens, and yeah, I'm a little disappointed, but I like her.

"Just Jules remember?"

"I am afraid not, my lady," she says, and offers me a knowing grin.

I bite my lip, and I nod.

What can I say?

But I refuse to be embarrassed.

Besides, Shade feels like the cool, unflappable BFF I never had.

She carries a silver tray and a folded bundle of what looks like more impossibly soft clothes.

"Lord Alaric bids you to break your fast, refresh yourself, and dress for the day."

I snort. "'Bids me'? Really?"

Shade's lips twitch. "Yes. He is waiting for you. He is taking you on a tour of Nightfall."

My eyebrows shoot up.

"He is?"

She nods, and for the first time in ages, I feel this sense of, I don't know what to call it, giddiness? Maybe.

Like a girl with a crush.

Like someone who might actually be someone else's crush.

And isn't that amazing?

For someone like Alaric to want me? Not for my utility. Not for convenience. But simply because I'm me.

Well, it's just too good to be true.

Definitely too good to waste on all the *what ifs*.

And honestly, I am so curious.

About him.

About this world.

About where this path might lead.

Even if it's all smoke and mirrors.

Even though I wonder if he'll get bored. If I'll be going home soon.

I think I'm ready to follow it just a little farther.

I grip the sheet tighter around me and rise from the bed, the silky fabric whispering against my skin.

"Okay then," I say, voice a little wobbly but getting stronger. "I guess I'd better get ready. Um, one question?"

Shade, ever composed, gives me a knowing grin. "Yes, Lady Jules?"

I wrinkle my nose. "Where's the bathroom?"

Her grin widens. "Ah. Right this way."

She doesn't walk toward a door—because there *isn't* one.

Not until she lifts a graceful hand and gestures toward the solid stone wall to my left.

Magic hums in the air. A low, living thrum.

And just like that, the wall *shifts*.

The bricks don't crumble or collapse—they *glide*, sliding apart in perfect precision, forming an elegant archway that glows faintly around the edges.

On the other side is, *well*, not just a bathroom.

It's a dream.

My jaw drops as I step inside, barefoot, sheet still clutched to my chest like armor.

The floor is a warm, pearlescent stone. It's smooth under my feet, but I can see it's etched with faint, glowing runes that pulse like a heartbeat.

To the right, an enormous sunken bath is built into the floor itself, filled by a cascading waterfall that flows from an opening high above in the arched ceiling.

But the water isn't just water.

It's *light*.

Shimmering like molten moonstone, scented faintly with something sweet.

Like jasmine and clove and magic.

Steam curls lazily in the air, sparkling as if it's laced with stars.

The room glows, but softly, without a single visible source of light. The stone walls breathe warmth, and everywhere I look, I see touches of beauty.

Flowers suspended mid-air in glass orbs, mirrors edged in silver that ripple like water, shelves stacked with thick, plush towels and glass bottles in every hue.

Shade gestures toward a smaller alcove with a discreet curtain.

"I trust you know what to do with these," she says, pointing to the very human toilet and—*oh God, yes*—a bidet.

My cheeks flare as I nod quickly.

"There is a new brush for your teeth," she continues, her voice gentle, "and this gel is our version of toothpaste. As for the bath, simply step inside. The waters of the Eyrie are enchanted—they will cleanse you thoroughly, without need for soaps or scrubbing. When you are finished, stand here." She points to a golden grate beside the tub. "The vent will warm and dry you instantly."

I blink at her. "Like a full-body hair dryer?"

"Something like that," she replies with a twinkle in her eye. "Oh, and here."

She walks to an elegant armoire that blooms open like a flower when she touches it.

Inside are lotions, oils, perfumes, ribbons, and even brushes made from bristles that shimmer like spun starlight.

"Are these for me?" I ask, my voice soft.

"Yes, Lady Jules. The Eyrie recognizes you now as Lord Alaric's *viyella* and will attend your needs and desires."

"Wow, this place is incredible," I whisper, my mind full of wonder.

She bows slightly, eyes suddenly more serious. "Magic lives in everything here. And you may find that it responds to you more than most, but I beg you, be careful, my lady. Not everything is as it seems in Nightfall."

I swallow and nod.

My fingers tighten around the edge of the sheet.

What did she say before her warning? The Eyrie *recognizes* me?

The idea of this ancient place having a cognition is frightening and wondrous. I make a mental note to ask Alaric about it.

"Take your time," Shade says, heading back

toward the doorway. "When you are ready, you'll find your gown waiting by the mirror and a tray with some pastries and tea."

"Oh, where will I find Alaric?"

"Do not worry, I will take you to him when you are ready."

And just like that, she disappears, the doorway sealing behind her with a gentle *click* that isn't mechanical—it's *sentient* somehow.

Like maybe the castle really is watching. Listening.

Maybe even welcoming me.

I turn back to the tub, the water glittering like moonlight melted into silk.

My heart thuds, loud in the quiet. But not afraid. Just awake.

I step forward, let the sheet fall, and descend into the warmth.

As I sink beneath the surface, something inside me unfurls.

It feels pleasant and alarmingly content.

Everyone I've met, *Alaric, Shade,* and everything I've seen so far, *mainly the Eyrie,* makes me feel like Nightfall is special.

Like I'm destined to be here.

Like it might be the home I've always yearned for.

And maybe, just maybe, I really do belong here.

CHAPTER 12
ALARIC

THE EYRIE—ROOFTOP

I feel like a green-as-grass boy waiting to see his first crush round the bend of a sunlit trail. It's absurd. I've faced down armies, ruled tempests, and outmaneuvered kings and monsters alike—but this?

This anticipation, this fluttering madness just beneath my ribs?

It's her.

Jules.

My viyella.

I know what's at stake.

I know Nightfall teeters on the edge of unraveling.

The SoulTakers are closing in.

The crown is hidden—*barely*.

The other Lords are restless.

Everything could crumble before moonrise.

And yet, I stand here like a fool on the wind-swept rooftop of the Eyrie, smoothing nonexistent wrinkles from my tunic, waiting for her.

Because today, I will do something I never thought I'd do.

I will shift into my Dragon form and take my *viyella* on a tour of our land.

The wind curls around me like a familiar pet, excited by my excitement.

Below, waterfalls crash into crystalline pools, silver mist rising like breath from the earth.

Forests stretch toward the horizon in shades of violet and jade, dotted with glowing fungi and creatures that exist only in this world.

From this perch—*my mountain throne*—the land is harsh, beautiful, wild. And today, it is hers to see.

The sound of footsteps breaks my reverie, and I glance toward the stairwell as Shade emerges first. Regal and composed as always, her fiery hair swaying like a banner.

And then—*thank the gods above and below*—she appears.

Myrrin. Jules.

Her dark hair is loose around her shoulders,

gleaming with whatever magic the Eyrie infused into her bath.

She wears a shorter, slate-blue dress made of silk that clings and flows in all the right places, cinched with a belt of braided silver.

Beneath it, she wears the supple leather leggings I sent—*hand-treated by my artisans to be soft against skin, but durable enough to protect her from the rub of scales.*

I had them made just for her. And I'd conjured a riding seat, too—woven from elemental silk and anchored with rune-locks.

It will rest between my wings, built for one rider. *Her.*

She approaches, looking up at me through thick lashes, cheeks pink from the mountain air—or perhaps from whatever she saw in my expression.

I clear my throat. "*Myrrin*, are you ready for an adventure?"

"Another one?" she quips, arching a brow. "I guess so. But I'm warning you, Alaric—" her voice lowers as she steps closer, eyes teasing "—a girl could get used to this."

"Good," I murmur, taking her hand and brushing my lips across her knuckles, "because I fully intend to get you very used to this."

She laughs softly, and the sound—*gods, the sound*—it echoes like wind chimes caught in a sunbeam. I swear I can feel my Dragon stir beneath my skin in response.

I guide her toward the open expanse of rooftop, where the wind howls in greeting.

The sky above is streaked with violet clouds, the sun in this realm a burnished gold.

The moment she steps up to the ledge, she gasps.

"Oh wow! It's—it's beautiful!"

The view is staggering. And I haven't even shown her me yet.

"Don't move," I say, and she looks at me curiously, but nods.

The wind answers my call before I give it voice.

The illusion I wore when I met her on Earth has already been done away with.

But now, it's this version of me that melts away in strips of light, revealing my other form.

This me is enormous, claws, scales, curling black horns, and the runes glowing down my skin like living fire.

My wings unfurl in one sweeping motion—*dark as obsidian, laced with streaks of lightning.*

My shift is painless, and fast. But I slow it down for her. So she may see.

The power of it shakes the stones beneath our feet.

My form expands exponentially—*muscle, magic, scale, and sinew*—until I am towering and magnificent, a great winged beast forged from air and shadow.

I glance down at her and see her awe.

No fear. Just wonder.

My heart thunders.

With great care, I lower myself, revealing the enchanted seat I conjured for her.

It's cradled between the ridges of my spine, secured by elemental binds no wind can loosen.

"Climb on, *my viyella*," I say, my draconian voice rumbling with a low, swirling growl that vibrates the air around us.

I could speak straight into her mind—*our bond allows that now*—but I resist.

She's still new to this world, new to me.

I don't want to overwhelm her more than I already have.

Still, the sight of her—*standing with the wind pulling at her dark hair, her cheeks flushed from the*

mountain air and what we shared last night—nearly undoes me.

She pauses, just for a breath. Then her lips lift into a grin that lights up the storm brewing in my chest. That smile could shatter kingdoms.

It could unravel me.

She approaches without fear, her eyes wide with wonder.

"Okay," she murmurs, more to herself than to me. "Let's do this."

Her hands brush along the curve of my scaled hide, reverent and curious, and I shiver beneath her touch.

Carefully, she climbs into the enchanted saddle I conjured between my wings, her weight settling onto me like a brand.

A little squeak of amazement escapes her lips.

It's fucking adorable.

I rise.

With one mighty push of my wings, we launch into the skies.

The wind greets me like an old friend, swirling around us, carrying our scents, our magic.

Clouds part, sunlight spills across the sky, and my brave little mortal clings to the reins I enchanted for her, her thighs tightening around my torso.

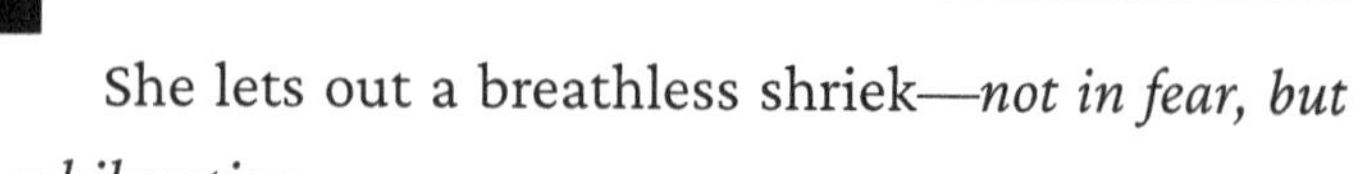

She lets out a breathless shriek—*not in fear, but exhilaration.*

A laugh bubbles from her lips. "Alaric! This is insane!"

In response, I tilt and roll, letting her feel the freedom of it. She clutches tighter and laughs louder, the sound echoing across the vast heavens.

"You're amazing!" she shouts into the roaring wind.

I answer her through our link, "Agree to disagree, *my viyella*, for it is you who amazes me."

Her gasp is audible, her joy crashing into me like a wave.

I feel it. Live it. Breathe it.

Magic hums between us, bending air, and making her shriek with joy.

I dare to ask, "Want to go faster?"

"Yes!" she cries aloud, her voice gleeful and daring.

And so I oblige.

I open my maw and let loose a stream of silver flame into the sky, branding the clouds with light.

Then I pull my wings tight, tucking them just so, and dive like a bullet.

We shoot across the horizon, faster than thought, slicing through the wind. Her thrilled cries

ride the air, wild and unafraid, and I feel her joy like fire beneath my skin.

I carry her higher—over the jagged mountains of the Eyrie, over the shimmer-laced forests and glassy rivers of Nightfall.

Creatures below lift their faces, sensing me. Knowing me. The Lord of Air, keeper of Winds, and now they know that I've claimed a mate.

But no one could know I've soul-bonded to this mortal. That I have indeed entered the zareth.

And for the first time in centuries, I feel it in my soul.

Freedom.

Because I'm not alone anymore.

I have her. *My viyella.* And I will never let her go.

CHAPTER 13
JULES

Alaric lands with a gentle thud, wings flaring wide before folding against his back like velvet shadows.

The ground quakes softly beneath his massive form, the scent of scorched wind and ancient power curling through the air.

The moment his Dragon touches the ground, I'm breathless. And not just from the flight, but from the place he's brought me to.

I don't know where to look first, so I look down. At my Dragon lover.

He's so big. Like really big.

I mean, hello? He's a mother-freaking Dragon.

But I don't scream. I don't faint. I don't run.

I just can't stop staring.

Because wow.

Just wow.

I should be used to this place by now.

This realm.

This magic.

The impossible beauty that seems to thread itself through every rock, every breeze, every word that slips from his lips.

But Alaric, in his full Draconian form?

That hits entirely different.

He is majesty carved from starlight.

Power born of the oldest myths.

Grace so staggering it steals the breath from my lungs.

His scales shimmer like liquid armor.

Like midnight threaded with silver, like someone gathered stardust and shadows and whispered life into them.

They ripple over him as he moves, catching the sunlight through the canopy above in dazzling bursts.

And then he turns. Slowly.

His majestic head swiveling toward me. Those eyes—*molten and intelligent*—find mine.

And everything in me stops.

Because he isn't just some mythical creature anymore.

He's him.

He's Alaric.

And he's looking at me like I'm his.

Like I'm something wondrous. Something rare.

Can you even imagine that?

Meeting an insanely hot guy who steals you from your home, brings you to another realm, turns into a creature of legend, and then looks at you like you're made of magic?

Oh my God. Do I sound nuts?

"Not at all. It is very astute of you, *Myrrin*," his voice rumbles through my mind—rich and deep, like thunder veiled in silk.

"All Dragons come from magic."

Of course they do.

"I knew it," I breathe aloud, clutching the leather straps that serve as makeshift reins.

"You're made of it. Nightfall. Stars. Fire, air, bone, flesh and something else. Something almost holy."

I pause and take a breath before saying aloud that thing I never dreamed I'd ever say.

"Magic is real."

He lets out a breath that stirs my hair, and the corners of his mouth curl in what I swear is a smile.

Or the Dragon version of one.

"Yes. And now you're part of it, too."

Me?

A part of this?

Something expands in my chest—*an ache I've carried for so long I didn't even know it had a name.*

He steps into a clearing at the edge of a secluded glade, his tail sweeping behind him like a banner.

His presence shakes the very trees.

Birds—*creatures that shimmer like crystal-laced finches*—flutter above.

Light dances off the pool beside us, fed by a waterfall so clear and bright it looks like it fell from the moon.

"Climb down, *my viyella*."

The way he says it. Like it means something special.

His voice, even like this, sinks into my bones and wraps around my heart.

That word—*viyella*—it sounds like a spell.

Like a sacred promise only the stars would dare witness.

And fool or not, I want to believe it.

I slide my leg over and begin to climb down, my

hands trailing over the smooth, warm scales of his flank.

They're sleek and solid beneath my palms, humming with energy.

"Smooth on the way down," he warns gently.

"But do not try from the other direction. My scales are armor. A defense. They would slice your delicate skin without meaning to."

I reach the ground and exhale, legs shaking from more than just the ride. I brush my hands down the leather leggings he had fashioned for me, enchanted to be warm and soft and protective.

"I hope you know," I say, daring a smile, "you've completely ruined me for all other men."

A low growl rumbles from deep within his chest.

"There are no other men for you," he growls, voice thick with dark certainty.

The air thrums in response, a subtle storm of want curling between us.

His next words feel like a thunderclap inside my soul.

"You are mine, *Myrrin*. And I swear to you, I don't share."

And maybe I should argue.

Maybe I should challenge that possessiveness.

But I don't want to.

Because somewhere in the wild, aching truth of me, I want to be his.

Entirely. Unapologetically.

The air charges again. Sparks flit across my skin, tingling with awareness.

And then, with a mighty growl, I watch as his form begins to change.

Scales dissolve into skin.

Wings tuck and fade.

Horns retract, becoming smaller, and dark waves of tousled hair tumble to his broad shoulders.

His muscles shift beneath golden-tan skin.

Ancient runes pulse faintly along his arms, his chest, and across his collarbones like branded whispers of his power.

He becomes Alaric again.

The man.

The Demon.

The Dragon tucked back inside, but still present.

He is all three at all times

All him.

And heaven help me—I think I'm already starting to fall in love with every part of him.

We're in a secluded glade, ringed by ancient trees whose silver leaves shimmer in the filtered light.

A waterfall spills from the jagged mouth of a cliff, its waters glowing a bright, impossible shade of teal.

The falls crash into a crystalline pool that stretches like a hidden gem across the mossy earth, steaming slightly with warmth.

Birdsong echoes through the air—only it's not birds, exactly.

I catch sight of creatures flitting between branches, their feathers glittering like crushed gemstones.

And down near the edge of the clearing, a fox-shaped animal curls in a patch of sun. Its fur ripples with threads of gold.

A little farther away, tiny critters, almost like bunnies, sniff around, nibbling on sweet grass.

"Are those, I mean, they look like?" I start, eyes wide.

"Those are some of the benevolent creatures of Nightfall," Alaric answers, his voice emoting power, but wrapped in velvet.

"You might see echoes of their Earthbound kin, but they carry the realm's magic in every hair and bone."

I watch as the fox lifts its head and stares back at

me with eyes too intelligent to be anything but sentient.

Then it yawns and returns to its nap.

"Wow," I whisper.

Alaric's gaze, however, is on me. And when I turn to meet it, I feel the shift.

We are alone here.

Completely.

The air thickens with something warm, heady, and unmistakable.

I glance at the pool tucked behind a cluster of massive boulders, a natural bath carved by the falls. It's partially hidden from the main glade, perfectly private.

Steam curls up from its surface, and the water glows faintly.

"Can we swim in there?" I ask, already imagining what it might feel like to slip in.

He dips his head, the corner of his mouth twitching with a barely there smile.

"Yes, if you like. These falls feed the Nightfall River. Its waters run through the entire realm. There is no purer current."

I step toward the pool, but I feel him mobbing behind me. It's unmistakably him.

His energy, his focus.

When I turn back, my breath catches.

Alaric is naked.

Like, completely naked.

One moment he was clothed in his billowy shirt and tight black pants—and the next?

Gone.

Just seven feet of muscled, tattooed, gorgeous male, standing there like temptation incarnate.

And then I feel it.

Cool air brushes across my own skin.

I look down, and yep.

No clothes.

"Oh my God," I gasp, covering myself as instinctively as I can with my hands and a twist of my hips.

Alaric's grin is wicked.

Unapologetic.

"You really have to warn a girl before you do that," I scold, trying to sound more offended than I feel.

Because truthfully?

I'm kind of thrilled.

Excited.

Heart pounding.

His eyes are fiery, drinking me in like I'm his next sin, and I shiver under the weight of that gaze.

"I could feel your curiosity," he says, his voice like midnight silk. "I merely acted on it."

"That's not how consent works," I mutter, but I'm smiling.

Blushing even though my pussy is clenching on air, my sex soaked with anticipation.

Alaric steps toward the water, and I follow— *because how could I not?*

With every breath I take, the magic of Nightfall seems to wrap tighter around my skin.

I'm glowing. Floating. And for the first time, I wonder if I was made for this place.

Or maybe this place was made for me.

CHAPTER 14
ALARIC

Thorn Mountain—The Secret Pool

The water inside the secret pool is warm, rising in curling steam as we sink into the hidden spring beside the falls.

The roar of the cascade is thunder in the distance, but here, in this tucked-away hollow surrounded by stone and trees, it feels private.

Protected.

Not enough.

With a silent breath, I call the winds.

They answer instantly, swirling around us in invisible currents, forming a barrier between our bodies and the rest of the world.

No eyes will see.

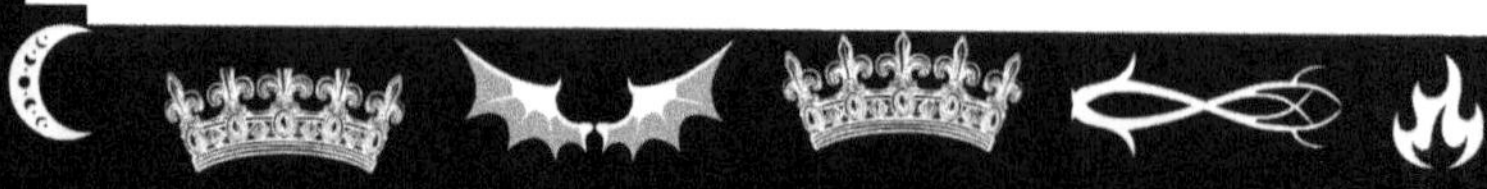

No ears will hear.

Not even the creatures of Nightfall will cross the veil I've cast.

She is mine. And I will not have any set their covetous eyes on her.

Does that make me a monster? Perhaps. But I'm surprisingly okay with that.

Jules leans back against the smooth rock, her hair damp, curling over her shoulder, her cheeks flushed from the heat of the water—or maybe from me.

She looks up at me with those wide, wondering eyes and smiles like I've given her the moon.

I haven't.

But I will.

"What just happened? It feels different," she whispers, and I lower myself into the water in front of her, watching her expression shift from coy to something more serious, something searching.

I cup her face, let my thumb trace her lower lip.

Gods, I want to devour her.

But first, she needs to understand.

"I called on my magic to create a barrier around us."

"Why?"

"Because if anyone else hears you," I murmur, my voice low, dangerous, "sees you like this—*soft, flushed, pliant in my arms*—I'll have to take their lives, *Myrrin*."

Her breath catches. The water laps softly against our skin.

"What? Why?"

"Because you are for my pleasure alone."

She raises a brow, that flirtatious curve of her lips returning, but I see past it. See through it.

"Is that all I am to you?" she asks softly. "Just something to take pleasure from?"

I hesitate.

Not because I don't know the answer.

But because I do.

And it terrifies me.

She is far more than I meant for her to be.

More than desire.

More than conquest.

More than I deserve.

But this game we play—*this edge of truth and temptation, illusion and reality*—it's too dangerous to name what she's becoming.

So I give her the only answer I can allow.

"You are *my viyella*."

The *zareth* pulses between us at the word.

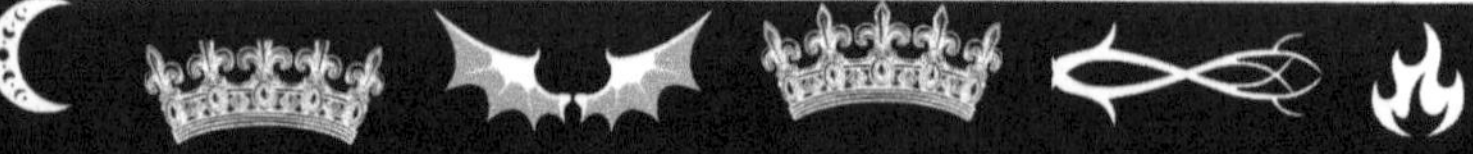

Ancient. Unyielding. Irrevocable.

And then I move.

In one fluid motion, I grab her hips and lift.

She gasps, clutching my shoulders, her thighs parting as I guide her over me.

I do not fumble. I do not search.

I find her—*exactly where I need to be*—with the first flex of my hips.

Her body opens for me, her cunt is wet and wanting, and the moment I slide deep into her heat, the world vanishes.

My vision tunnels.

My breath stops.

She moans, a soft sound swallowed by the cocoon of magic we're wrapped in.

"Alaric," she whispers like prayer.

I don't answer.

I just hold her tighter.

And begin to move.

Cupping her ass, I grind against her clit, loving the way her pussy rewards me with a squeeze every time I stroke her just right.

And I can't stop.

I don't want to.

I drive into her, deeper, faster, touching her everywhere I can.

Her legs lock around my waist like shackles made of silk and sin.

Thick thighs squeezing, hips lifting greedily to meet every slow, deliberate thrust I give her.

And fuck, the sounds she makes—*each gasp, moan, and whimper*—is its own kind of spell.

I lick into her mouth, tasting her pleasure, swallowing her need, refusing to give her air because I want to feel her pulse against my tongue.

I want to own her in every breath, every beat.

But my viyella?

She just clutches me tighter.

She takes me like she was made for me.

Like her body was carved by the same gods who wrote our bond in the stars.

And it undoes me.

I'm barely holding on, but still, I want more.

Truth is, I want everything.

This started as a means to an end. An illusion I thought I could conjure like any glamour I've ever cast.

But I'm in over my head. I fucking know it. And it's way too late to stop now.

And even if it causes me to lose focus and Nightfall suffers? I think it might be worth it.

I slow my hips, dragging each thrust until she trembles.

She whines, pleading with her body, her hands fisting my hair.

But I'm not done teasing her yet.

Lowering my head, I wrap my lips around one aching, perfect nipple, suckling her like she's the only sustenance I've ever known.

She arches beneath me, hips bucking.

"Please," she begs, and it is like music to my ears.

Sweet shadows, she tastes like heat and lightning.

Like the promise of chaos and eternity.

My *Myrrin* is my favorite fucking flavor. And I intend to savor every bite.

"Oh God," she moans, ragged and real.

I answer with my teeth.

A sharp nip—*just enough to make her flinch*.

To make her feel me.

"Say my name when I fuck you, *viyella*," I growl, voice roughened with possession.

She gasps again, trying to rock her hips, but I hold her in place, hand firm on her waist.

"Your name?" she pants. "You call me *Myrrin*, and v-something. Who even knows what!"

I pause, pulling back enough to meet her eyes. They glitter, defiant and wet with heat.

Gods, I love her fire.

"My name," I repeat, grinding my hips just enough to make her eyes flutter before I stop and back off a bit.

"I want you to fall apart screaming it."

She stares at me, narrowing her gaze.

That spark in her isn't fading. No, it's catching fire.

"Compromise," she breathes, lashes low, lips swollen. "What's something I can say, a male nickname for whatever you call me?"

Her question hits me like a lightning strike.

Unexpected. Perfect.

"Viyen."

The word escapes before I think. Before I can guard against it.

An ancient title.

A sacred one.

Not lightly spoken.

Not ever.

"Is that what you are to me?" she whispers, voice thick with wonder, hands rising to press flat against my chest—right over the pounding of my traitorous heart.

I thrust deeper, slower, sealing my mouth to hers in a kiss that's pure possession.

Little minx that she is, she snakes her hand up my spine, caressing my hair, then up further till she is stroking my horns.

Fuck me. My cock gets harder.

I pull back, but I don't stop her. My lips are brushing hers as I answer, honest and raw and wrecked, "Yesss," I hiss, unable to rein in the beast within me.

"I am your *viyen*. As you are my *viyella*."

"That sounds permanent," she whispers, eyes wide and mesmerizing.

"It is, Jules Strano. You may not know what this all means yet, but I know you can feel it. In your body. In your bones. In your human heart and soul. Tell me you do."

"I do, *viyen*," she whimpers, stroking my horns now, and gods be damned, I am burning for her. "I feel it."

"Mine," I snarl, slamming my mouth to hers, driving my cock inside her tight heat in time with my tongue.

And then, I give her what she needs.

What I need.

I fuck her like I'm the storm and she's the lightning rod.

Like I was forged for this moment. For this woman. For our bond.

The zareth wraps around our bodies like a cord.

And as her walls clamp down, and her cries fill the barrier of wind and magic, I know with bone-deep certainty, I am keeping my viyella.

No matter the cost.

CHAPTER 15
JULES

The North Village Market smells like spices and bread and something sweet I can't name but absolutely want to try.

Sunlight is filtering through the emerald canopy hanging over the outer fringes of the square. The forests here are wild.

But that sunlight? It's gold and red and it glimmers off everything, making even the worn cobblestones look magical.

Shade walks beside me, her luminous gray skin catching the light in an ethereal way.

She is vibrant and the village is bustling, filled with sound and scent and color, and she walks beside me like she owns the place.

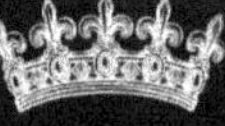

Her long red braid sways behind her, gleaming like firelight in the sun, and her steps are confident, her chin lifted with quiet pride.

"This way, Lady Jules," she says with a sly smile, pointing out a row of covered booths arranged in a crescent.

"That one sells *flamefruit*—don't eat the seeds unless you like breathing smoke. And those are *chitter melons*. Sweet, but they hum when they ripen."

I blink at the pink-striped orbs stacked in perfect pyramids.

Sure enough, they vibrate faintly, giving off a musical, almost giggling sound as we pass.

"Try this," Shade says, pressing a tiny square of something golden into my palm. It smells nutty and sweet, like a baked good and a candy bar had a baby.

I pop it in my mouth and close my eyes, humming in pleasure.

"Oh my God."

"It is the cream produced after pressing baoba beans and grinding the paste together with nuts and fruits for sweetness and flavor," she says, proud as punch.

I nod, mouth still full.

"I'm not going to lie, this is incredible. It tastes like a peanut butter cup."

I moan a little, missing all things Reese's with the kind of bone-deep ache only sugar withdrawal can cause.

I reach for a second sample. This one's a pretty lavender cube from a fancy tray on the other end of the cart.

"What does this taste like?" I ask, holding it up for inspection.

Shade gasps, smacking the cube from my hand so fast I stumble backward.

"No! You mustn't eat that, Lady Jules!"

"What? Why?!"

"That," she says gravely, "is poison."

I blink at the fallen cube like it's a snake.

"Poison?! It's just sitting there!"

"Indeed," she nods solemnly. "The scent keeps rodents and wing-thieves away. It is safe to touch, but even the smallest bite would kill you—*and me*—within seconds."

"Geezus. Okay. No purple poison cube of death. Got it."

I wipe my hand on my dress and glance nervously at the shopkeeper, who looks somewhere between horrified and deeply apologetic.

Shade bows quickly and mutters a few words in what I think is the local tongue.

The woman relaxes, offering me a brittle smile and a free pouch of baoba cream.

Shade takes my elbow.

"Come. There is a flower stand just beyond the fountain I think you will like."

I follow, still shaken, but curious. The air here smells like bread and herbs and morning dew.

Soft flute music plays from somewhere I can't see, and despite the near-death by cube, this market is kind of magical.

The flower stand?

Absolutely blows me away.

I gasp, actually gasp, at the sight before me. "Are these real?"

Hundreds of flowers crowd the wooden stall and its shelves, spilling onto baskets and crates in every imaginable color—and then some.

I see familiar blooms like tulips and roses, but also others with glowing petals or pulsing centers that change hue with the shifting breeze.

A hanging vine shivers as I approach, and one of its fuzzy violet fronds reaches toward me.

"Is it waving?" I whisper.

"They are curious," Shade says. "And not technically plants, though we call them flowers for ease. That one enjoys warmth. Offer your wrist."

Tentatively, I extend my arm. The frond curls around it gently, tickling my skin.

"Oh wow. This is weirdly soothing."

"It likes you," she says, clearly amused.

"Okay, note to self: don't eat the poison cubes, but make friends with the sentient flowers."

Shade laughs, and it's the most relaxed I've seen her all morning.

"You adjust quickly."

"I don't think I have a choice."

Everything is alive here.

The colors are brighter.

The air is sweeter.

The sky stretches wide and crystalline blue above us, ringed by the towering spires of the mountains surrounding the Eyrie like ancient guardians.

And the people?

They look mostly human. But Shade's words keep echoing in my mind.

They're not.

"They remind me of regular boys back home," I murmur, nodding toward a group of teens loitering near a jewelry stand, their gazes locked on me like I've sprouted antlers.

Shade follows my line of sight and tsks. "Some of the young ones are changelings. You must be wary, Lady Jules. Spies for the SoulTakers come in many forms."

I go still. "Spies? Kids?"

"They are not children," she says simply, voice going cold. "Not truly. SoulTakers twist what they touch."

I nod slowly, not fully understanding, but not ready to question her either.

She leads me to a fabric stall next, where bolts of shimmering cloth ripple in the breeze like living creatures.

I run my fingers across one the color of moonlight and gasp at the way it shifts with my mood—*turning faintly lavender when I smile.*

"The market is safe today," Shade says gently, as if sensing my unease. "But it is not wrong to encourage caution. Nightfall is beautiful, yes. But it is also layered. Dangerous. And ever changing."

"Like its people," I murmur, watching a woman with eyes like flame barter with a merchant whose skin shifts between ice and coal.

Shade hums in agreement. "We call ourselves Demons, but we are not, as your world defines the word. No more good or evil than the average human, I suppose."

"Have you been reading about my world?" I ask, having found some volumes about Earth in the library.

I'm delighted she's taken an interest since, really, I could use a friend here. Alaric has many duties, and we can't be together all the time.

Even that worries me.

My desire to just be with him. I've never felt anything like it before.

"Yes, I have read some volumes in order to better understand you," she says and blushes.

"I hope that's not the only reason. I don't need you to be my servant," I begin, going for it. "I'd rather you be my friend."

"Friend?" her eyebrows go sky high. Then she narrows her gaze and nods solemnly. "I would like that very much, Lady Jules."

"Just Jules," I reply and grin, bumping her playfully with my shoulder.

She doesn't know how to react, but when I smile, she does the same and we start walking again.

"Tell me about your people," I say, pausing to admire some pottery for sale at another stand.

"Okay. Well, some among us are born with gifts. Magic. Power. But that is mostly seen in the Highborn, like Lord Alaric. Others—*like me*—have limitations to what magic we can use. We simply serve Nightfall, work to survive, and try to stay out of the wars of greater things."

"Alaric is Highborn?" I whisper, the name slipping from my lips like a secret.

"Indeed, he is more than just Demon," she confirms. "He is also Dragon. An ancient kind. And powerful beyond measure."

"I've seen his Dragon. Can everyone do that here?"

"You've seen Lord Alaric's Dragon?" she says, stopping in her tracks head tilted.

"Yeah, we went out the other day. I rode on his back, or neck, I suppose," I mumble.

"He let you ride him?"

She seems stunned and I don't know if I've said something wrong or told a secret I shouldn't have spilled.

"Um, it's no big deal, Shade. He just took me for a ride," I murmur and shrug.

"It is a very big deal, Lady Jules," she whispers and drops her gaze and her head. Almost like she is bowing to me.

"What are you doing?"

"You really are his fated mate, aren't you? The true *viyella* to our Lord," she says, bowing again, and this time when she raises her head, her cheeks are wet with tears.

"W-what do you mean?"

"I apologize, my lady. It is for Lord Alaric to tell you. Come, let us continue to stroll," she says.

I swallow hard, that little thrill of fear and wonder tangling in my chest again.

It's overwhelming. This place. These people. Him.

And me? I'm just a girl from Earth.

But as I trail my fingers over a lace shawl that shimmers like frost and listen to Shade hum a lullaby in a language older than anything I know, I feel it again.

That whisper of belonging.

Frightening. Strange. And somehow impossible not to want.

There are so many people out, and after the whole bowing thing, many of them are staring.

And I don't know why, but today feels important.

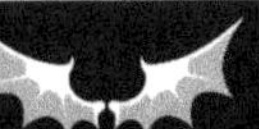

CHAPTER 16
JULES

I know it's market day.

But more importantly, according to Shade, it's *Ask Day*.

"Tell me what today is again," I say, trying not to react to the stares and whispers.

"Yes, of course. Ask Day is a time of year, usually held every quarter, when our people present Lord Alaric with their grievances, needs, and requests for his judgment," she says matter-of-factly.

"What kind of problems?" I ask, brushing my fingers over bolts of lace and soft, silken linen at a vendor's table.

A sweet-looking older woman smiles at me, and

her daughters giggle when I compliment the pale blue embroidery.

"Anything, Lady Jules. Disputes between neighbors. Land boundaries. A cartwheel needing replacement. Even matchmaking requests."

"Wait," I stop walking and smile so hard it hurts. "Alaric is a matchmaker?"

Shade tilts her head, confused. "Not exactly. But it is the dream of many villagers to have their Lord bless their unions. Especially during Ask Day. Do they not do that on Earth?"

"Not unless you count dating apps," I laugh. "Some cultures still use matchmakers, but not really anymore. Back home, people want to meet someone who just gets them. Someone to fall in love with."

"Strange," she murmurs, brows knitting.

I snort. "You're telling me. But it's supposed to be about connection. Not sex or dowries or parental approval."

She doesn't reply immediately, and the silence stretches just long enough to make me glance over. Shade's expression is unreadable. Thoughtful.

"So, people ask him for matchmaking?" I press.

"Yes. Especially now. Since you arrived."

"How do you mean?" I ask her.

"There's been talk," Shade says quietly.

I glance over at her. The wind teases her red braid over one shoulder, and she doesn't meet my eyes at first.

"What kind of talk?" I ask.

She finally looks at me then, and there's something unreadable in her expression.

A weight.

A warning.

Her eyes, normally the color of polished ash, seem to darken with whatever truth she's holding back.

"About the prophecy," she says.

I stop walking. "What prophecy?"

Shade sighs, as if she regrets bringing it up at all —*but the words spill anyway, like they've been waiting to be said.*

"In Nightfall, the realm is ruled by the great Lords. Each commands a dominion carved out by old power and older bloodlines. Lord Alaric rules the Eyrie and all the wild lands west of the Thorn Mountains. His brethren—*Lords Kael, Thorne, and Dagan*—govern their own territories. Together, they kept the realm in balance. Until," she pauses.

"Until what?"

"The Prime fell," she says softly. "The fifth Lord.

The one who ruled over all. He died in battle, and with him, the balance broke."

I swallow, heart thudding. "And this prophecy?"

Shade glances around, as if wary of ears even here, on the market path.

Her voice lowers. "It is said that each Lord inherits his true power only when he finds his mate. Not just a lover or consort. *A viyella*. When a zareth bond forms, it is unbreakable. Something older than blood. Older than Nightfall itself."

"A *zareth*," I repeat. "I think that's what Alaric mentioned when we—" I trail off.

Her eyes widen.

"It is a rare thing, my lady—I mean, *Jules*. Sacred. It binds two souls. And when that bond is true, it awakens something ancient. Magic reborn. They say the right bond could even elevate a Lord to Prime."

I blink at her. "Wait. So, you're saying if Alaric formed this zareth bond with me, he could become the new Prime?"

Shade hesitates.

"That's what the old legends say," she admits. "But," again she pauses.

"But?"

"You're human, Lady Jules. We've never had a human bonded to a Lord. Some whisper it's impossible. That the zareth can't form with someone from your world. That you're just a distraction or an illusion like so many our Lord creates."

"Illusion?"

"Yes. One of Lord Alaric's many titles. Something his magic is infamous for. He is the Lord of Illusion."

A cold ache forms in my chest.

"So, Alaric is the Lord of Air and Illusion, and you all think I'm just in the way," I say slowly. "Or worse, that I'm a tool."

"Oh, my lady, no, I did not mean—"

"Please," I whisper. "Friends don't lie, Shade. Even when the truth hurts."

Shade doesn't answer. She doesn't have to.

Her silence says enough.

I look up toward the Eyrie, where I know Alaric is still holding court, hearing the pleas of his people like some kind of otherworldly king with wings and glowing skin and a voice that can shatter me in one breath and rebuild me in the next.

A mate. A zareth. A prophecy that could change everything.

And here I am.

A girl from Earth with a messy past, an ache for belonging, and a Dragon Lord who looks at me like I might be more.

But what if I'm not?

What if I'm just distracted by the illusion he created?

What if I'm simply the means to his end?

Her words hit like a stone dropped into still water.

Unimaginable strength.

Magic reborn.

The words replay over and over in my brain.

And all I can think is—was I stolen from my home for that reason?

Did he see me and think *power* instead of *person*?

Shade says nothing more, only tugs me toward a vendor offering candied nuts wrapped in gold-dusted parchment.

But my appetite has dulled.

And for the first time since arriving in Nightfall, I feel a chill creep up my spine that has nothing to do with the weather.

The path that leads to the meeting place winds through the village and up a small hill, where sunlight pierces the clouds that have risen suddenly.

It's just enough to bathe everything in a golden haze.

I walk beside Shade, trying to focus on the beauty around me and not the whirring in my head.

Was I stolen because Alaric truly wanted me? Or am I being used in his power play?

Shade hums a little as we approach the central green, where the villagers have gathered in a wide circle.

At the center, elevated on a platform of stone and twisted silver roots, I see *him.*

Alaric.

The sight of him steals the breath from my lungs.

He's perched on something that looks like a throne, though I'm not sure it was built so much as *grown* from the magic that is Nightfall.

Intricate glyphs glow across his bare forearms and along the V of his chest, where his shirt hangs open.

His wings—*those impossible black-and-silver things*—are relaxed, but even at rest, they seem powerful enough to stir storms.

A Lord in every sense of the word.

And something more.

There's a quiet reverence in the crowd as he speaks to the last of the day's petitioners.

It's a young woman with a child tucked into her skirts, nervously wringing her hands. I can't hear their words, but I see how he leans forward, how intently he listens.

Then, with a gesture of his hand, the woman gasps, bows low, and backs away.

Alaric speaks again—this time to an attendant who quickly disappears with a nod.

He looks up then.

Looks *right at me.*

And for a second, everything else disappears.

The people, the village, even Shade at my side.

It's just him.

And me.

My chest aches with something I don't understand. Want, maybe. Or hope.

Or maybe both.

Shade turns to speak with another attendant, giving me space.

Alaric's attention is summoned by his people, and he drops his gaze.

Though, maybe he does it reluctantly? Like he doesn't want to stop looking at me.

I stand quietly, not wanting to intrude, watching him like he's the last page of a story I'm desperate to read again.

Until I'm no longer alone.

"Quite the image, isn't he?" a deep, accented voice says from somewhere behind me.

I stiffen and turn, just enough to see a man standing far too close. He's tall, muscular, with dark hair braided back and ink crawling over the side of his face and neck in swirling, unfamiliar patterns.

His eyes—a color I've never seen on a man, all fire and shades of red and orange—gleam with knowing.

"Are you fooled by the illusion you see before you, human?"

My spine straightens. "Excuse me?"

He smiles, and it isn't friendly.

"Lord Alaric in all his glory," he says, gesturing toward the throne with mockery dripping from his voice. "But do you really believe that is who he is? A benevolent ruler? A noble protector?"

I frown. "He *is* their Lord. They respect him."

"Respect," he sneers, "is not love. And love is not something he is capable of. Not the kind you seek, anyway."

That hits a little too close.

"I don't know what you think you know," I snap, "but—"

"Oh, I *know*," he cuts in smoothly. "You want

him to love you. You want him to choose you. But his heart already has a master."

The words land like stones.

"Nightfall," he says softly. "It owns him. It always has."

I look toward the platform again. Alaric is still seated there, head tilted slightly as he doles out favors and grants petitions to his subjects.

"If you want his love," the stranger whispers, stepping closer, "I'm afraid, little human, you will never get it."

A chill moves through me. One I can't explain.

But before I can respond—*before I can demand who he is or how he knows any of this*—he's gone.

Just gone.

Shade returns a moment later, but I barely register her presence. Because something inside me has started to crack.

And I don't know if I can survive what might be on the other side.

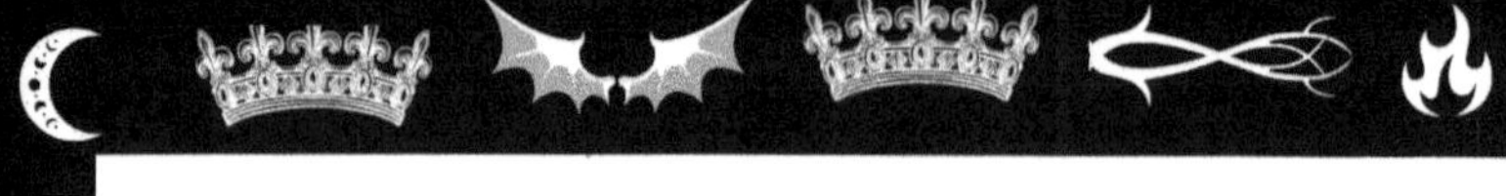

CHAPTER 17
ALARIC

THE EYRIE—DINING ROOM

Night blankets the Eyrie in velvet shadows, the stars glittering just beyond the open balcony.

I've cast warming spells on the breeze, but the chill I feel tonight has nothing to do with the wind.

Jules didn't touch her dinner.

She'd smiled politely, even nodded when I poured her wine, but her mind was elsewhere.

Far from me.

Far from us.

And now she stands in front of one of my most sacred tapestries. She's silent. Distant.

Her expression is unreadable as firelight dances across her features.

My chest aches.

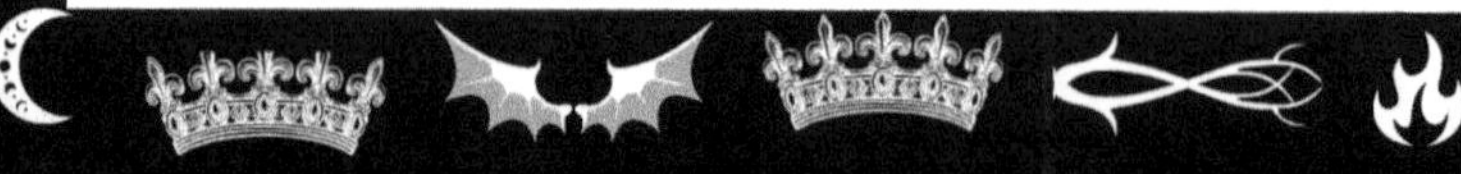

She spent all afternoon at the North Village Market with Shade, and I'd hoped the day would lift her spirits.

Some of the merchants told me she was sweet, warm, even funny.

I came back to find the entrance of my keep overflowing with their admiration.

Gifts of lace and honeyed fruits, fragrant oils and handwoven charms, all wrapped, and all addressed to the *Lady of the Eyrie.*

And stars help me, I was proud.

Proud she was mine.

Even if this was never the plan.

Even if I should have kept my distance.

Even if I'm starting to crave her happiness more than that damned crown.

My voice is gentler than I expect when I ask, "Are you feeling well, *Myrrin*?"

She doesn't look at me.

Her gaze stays fixed on the tapestry.

The one woven with shadow-thread and light-silk, depicting the final moments of the last Unicorn of Nightfall.

Jules tilts her head slightly, voice barely a whisper.

"This tapestry makes me feel sad. But I don't understand it. What is it showing me, Alaric?"

I move to stand beside her, keeping a careful distance.

Close enough to feel her warmth.

Far enough not to spook her.

"It's showing the last of the mystical horned beasts of Nightfall. A Unicorn," I begin, and even saying the word hurts.

She finally glances at me, her brows drawing together.

"In our realm, the Unicorn was not just a creature. It was hope. Dreams. Innocence made flesh. The SoulTakers believed that killing it would end dreaming in the multiverse. That all realms would fall to darkness without the Unicorn's light."

Her eyes fill with tears, and fuck me, I can't bear it. I curl my hands into fists, my claws digging into my palms.

Her lips part. "Did it?"

I shake my head slowly.

"No. Because even though the beast died, its spirit did not. That is the great lie the SoulTakers never understood. You can kill a body, but not a dream. Not truly."

She looks back to the tapestry, and I sense the tremble in her aura.

"So the Unicorn lives on?" she asks, her voice tight with something I can't name.

"In a way. In Nightfall, we say the Unicorn's soul scattered like stardust, finding its way into the hearts of those brave enough to believe in impossible things."

My voice is so low now. A whisper. A breath, really.

A beat of silence passes between us.

Then, quieter than before, she says,

"Someone at the market told me you're not capable of love. That your heart only beats for the c-crown."

My jaw tightens.

The words cut deeper than I expect.

I've endured blades, betrayal, loss that would hollow out lesser men.

But this?

This shatters something fragile inside me. Something I didn't even know I was protecting.

Anger rises, hot and fast. My vision bleeds crimson at the edges.

A stranger approached my viyella?

My mate.

My only.

I had guards stationed. I'd tasked Shade with watching over her.

And still, someone slipped through.

Someone close enough to whisper poison in her ear.

Close enough to harm her.

To look into her soft, open face and lace doubt into her heart.

And gods forgive me, he did harm her.

Not with fists or flame.

But with words sharp as razors, slicing into the bond we've barely begun to form.

I take a step forward.

Then another.

I can't keep my distance. I don't want to.

I don't even know what I'll say. I only know I have to say something.

Anything.

My voice is low and rough, like gravel underfoot.

"I've made many mistakes, Jules."

She flinches almost imperceptibly at that.

But I see it.

I feel it.

"I've lied. I've manipulated. I've used my power to create illusions. And yes, I brought you here with an agenda that served only me. A claim that I told myself was just strategy. Just politics."

I exhale, forcing myself to hold her gaze.

"But it's not that anymore. And I can't stomach pretending otherwise."

Her eyes shimmer in the firelight, wide and uncertain. I want to fall to my knees and kiss that doubt from her brow.

"You have questions, *Myrrin*? Then ask," I beg her.

"Don't let anyone else tell you what I am," I continue, my voice vibrating with magic and emotion. "Or what I feel. You want the truth?"

She nods once, her lips parting slightly.

I take another step, the space between us dwindling to nothing.

"Why me?" she whispers, tears spilling onto her soft cheeks, and I can't bear it.

"It could only ever be you," I whisper, kissing those tears away.

Her breath hitches.

Her heart pounding, echoing like a war drum in my head.

"I need you, Jules. I crave you. Your voice. Your fire. Your maddening, beautiful spirit that refuses to bow, even when you should. I wanted

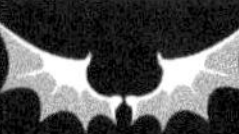

power. I wanted the crown. And then I met you."

My hands are on her neck and throat, cradling, caressing.

I tilt her head, so her beautiful, amber-colored eyes are looking at me.

I swallow hard.

The words catch.

"And now? Now I want things I should never want. Things no Lord of Nightfall dares to dream. And none of them have a damn thing to do with a throne."

She doesn't speak.

Doesn't blink.

Just breathes. A shallow, silent, shaking breath.

I drop my hands from her throat, then I lift one, brushing my knuckles down her cheek.

She leans into it, and that small act unravels me.

"I'm not sorry I stole you," I say, voice like a prayer or a curse—*I don't know which*. "I'm not sorry I brought you here. Or claimed you. Or made you mine in every way I could."

My hand moves to her neck, thumb brushing the place where my bite still pulses faintly with residual magic.

"I'm only sorry I didn't deserve you when I did."

Silence falls between us.

Not awkward.

Not empty.

Just charged with tension. *With truth.*

And then she whispers, "Do you deserve me now?"

I stare at her for a heartbeat too long.

Then I answer, with all the steel and softness I have, "I'm trying."

Her eyes finally rise to mine.

There's confusion in them.

Hurt.

Maybe even hope.

"I don't want to be used," she whispers. "Not by you. I won't survive it."

Gods, her words gut me.

"You are not a pawn," I say. "You are the one thing in all the worlds I cannot seem to control. And for that, I am more grateful than you will ever know."

She sways closer.

I swear the air crackles.

"I don't know what I am to you, Alaric," she says, "but I know what you're becoming to me. And it scares the hell out of me."

I touch her cheek again, cupping the face I know I can't live without.

"Then let us be afraid together."

She leans into my palm.

And for the first time in a thousand years, I feel like something ancient and broken inside me has begun to heal.

"My viyella," I whisper.

Then I claim her mouth.

There's no hesitation.

No battle of wills.

She meets me with heat and hunger, arms winding around my neck as she opens for me.

Her lips, her heart, her soul.

Gods, she tastes like hope.

Like fire and sweetness and something I've never had but always wanted.

My hands slide down her back, gripping her plump ass with a need I no longer try to hide.

I want her close. Closer.

Until there is no space, no air, no past between us.

Only now. Only this.

I growl deep in my chest, casting wards to shut the dining room off from servers and attendants.

I need her now, and I will not share a single breath this woman takes with anyone else.

Not when we are like this.

Not when we are together.

Jules moans into the kiss, the sound guttural and soft at once.

My stomach tightens and my blood roars.

Her hands explore, threading through my hair, coasting over my horns—*naughty minx.*

"Not yet," I growl, nipping her lip.

She whimpers, dragging them down to the runes etched across my skin.

They glow beneath her touch, responding to her as if they recognize her as mine.

As if the magic of Nightfall itself bends to her now, because she is *my viyella.*

Mine.

I lift her up, wrapping her legs around my waist as she gasps in surprise. Her back hits the wall, but she barely feels it.

My magic cushions the impact, casting a whisper of wind and warmth between her skin and the stone.

Then I drop to my knees.

"What are you—fuck, Alaric!" she moans, voice

catching as her dress evaporates in a shimmer of spell-light, falling away like mist.

I wrench her thighs open with reverent force, pressing kisses along the soft, trembling skin before fastening my mouth to her dripping pussy.

Gods, she's divine.

I moan into her as I lick through her folds, tasting her sweetness, her salt, her surrender.

Every flick of my tongue is worship. Every breath she takes, a sacred sound.

She gasps as I circle her clit, then dips her hips toward me with helpless instinct.

Her channel tightens as I slide my tongue deeper, seeking the source of her heat.

My hands grip her thighs, but I can feel her squirm, desperate for something to hold on to.

She reaches back, palms searching for purchase, but I won't let her fall.

Not ever.

I tighten the magic supporting her, making sure she's suspended in pleasure, not pain. The wall may be cold and ancient, but my power makes it a throne for her alone.

Mine. My viyella. My queen.

When I replace my tongue with two fingers,

thrusting into her slick heat, her cries grow louder, more frantic.

Her pussy clenches tight, as if she doesn't want to let me go.

"You're so beautiful when you fall apart, *Myrrin*," I groan, fucking her slow and deep with my fingers. "I want to see it. I want you to tell me when it happens."

Her eyes lock with mine, pupils blown wide.

Her lips part, and my name escapes in a breathless moan.

"Alaric, please," she whines, and the sound is nirvana.

"Tell me," I demand, my voice like gravel. "I want to hear what I do to you. Tell me how I make you feel, *Myrrin*. Now."

I pinch her clit gently. But firm enough to pull a gasp from her lips, then roll it between two fingers while I curl the others inside her.

My pinky teases the edge of her tight little ass, claws retracted. This touch is not about pain.

Not tonight.

Tonight is pleasure. Only pleasure.

I lower my mouth to her again, tongue working in tandem with my hands. She cries out louder, fists

tangling in my hair as her thighs spread wider for me.

"Feels so good. You feel so good. Please, don't stop," she whimpers, raw and undone. Her voice shreds what's left of my restraint.

"Call me your *viyen*," I growl against her thigh, the word thick with longing. "Here. Now. I want to hear you claim me like you did at the spring. Tell me I'm yours. I want to be yours."

I suckle her clit, tongue fluttering with purpose, and she comes undone in my mouth—*shaking, gasping, calling out.*

"Yes, you're mine, Alaric. My viyen. Fuck, like that—yes!"

Her head tips back, lips parted, flushed and radiant as she rides the high I give her.

That right there?

That is my favorite sight in all the realms. Jules, completely wrecked by my touch, with my name on her lips and my title bound to her breath.

When her spasms ease, and she returns to herself, her gaze finds mine.

She's still trembling, still panting.

But her fingers cradle my face with exquisite tenderness.

"Alaric," she whispers. "Viyen."

My name, my role, my truth. Spoken in her voice, it becomes holy.

"Yes. Yours, *Myrrin*. And now," I growl, rising to my feet in one smooth motion, "I take what's mine."

Her legs lock back around me, and with one thrust of my hips, I sink into her heat.

She's soaked, welcoming, clinging to me like a lifeline.

We both gasp—*one breath, one body.*

With a flick of magic, the dining room vanishes, fading into mist.

The world bends and reshapes to our desire.

We land together on the bed, the silken sheets cool against fevered skin.

And then I move.

Each thrust is deep and deliberate, hips snapping forward as I brace one hand behind her head, the other gripping her hip to hold her steady.

She cries out with every drive of my cock, meeting me thrust for thrust, body writhing beneath mine.

Another push, another roll of our hips together —*and I swear we scatter stars.*

They burn in our blood. In her screams. In my roar.

We don't just come—*we ignite.*

And as we fall, wrapped in magic and sweat and each other, I know one thing for certain.

There is no more illusion, no more deceit between us.

Whoever that bastard at the market was, he didn't break us apart. He pushed us closer together.

Jules is my viyella.

And I am her viyen.

She lies bare beneath me, sated and breathless. Radiant in her honesty. Her lush curves bare and glistening with sweat.

She is irresistible.

Her breasts rise with each breath, nipples peaked, skin flushed.

"So beautiful," I whisper. "By the stars, Jules, you are magnificent."

I kiss down her neck, her collarbone, the valley between her breasts.

This time I will go slow. Take my time. Taste and adore every inch of her like only I will ever do.

Her hands fist in the sheets, her body arching for more.

And I give it.

I trail lower, over the soft curve of her belly, down to the wet, waiting heat between her thighs.

She gasps when I part her folds with my fingers, slick and eager for me.

I sink two fingers inside her, slow and deep, curling them just right—and gods, the way she writhes.

"More," she begs, voice cracking. "*Viyen,* please."

I growl low in my throat. "Say it again."

"*Viyen.*"

I can't get enough of hearing her say that.

Lust and love twist together, and I lose the last thread of my restraint.

I rise above her, letting her see all of me.

My scars, my power, the hunger in my eyes.

My cock is thick and ready, flushed dark with need.

She reaches for me, eyes wide with trust.

And I slide inside her in one smooth, deep thrust.

We cry out together, her walls gripping me tight, like her body knows mine, like we were made for this.

I rock into her slowly at first, each stroke dragging pleasure through both our bodies until she's clawing at my back, whispering my name like a chant.

Her nails rake over my shoulders.

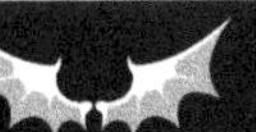
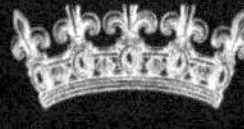

My rune-marked hands grip her hips, guiding her as we move together.

Not just fucking.

Claiming.

Her breath shatters.

Her body tenses, shivering on the edge.

"I've got you," I promise. "Come for me, *Viyella.*"

She does—*with a cry that echoes through the stone walls, her magic exploding with mine in a storm of silver fire.*

I follow, roaring her name as I spill inside her, stars crashing behind my eyes.

I feel it. And I know she does. Our bond. Our *zareth*, tightening, almost burning in its intensity.

We collapse together, breathless, tangled in each other.

And when I feel the lingering heat pulse between our hearts again, steady and sure, I know the truth I've been avoiding.

This has never been part of a strategy.

This has always been about us. Jules and me. Bound forever.

And when I open my eyes, I'm astounded.

"Your—your hair," I murmur, seeing her once dark locks laced now with the stars themselves.

And I know she is a blessing.

CHAPTER 18
JULES

"Oh my fuck! My hair. What is going on with my hair? ALARIC!"

That's the first thing out of my mouth once I can string two coherent thoughts together after Alaric rocks my entire nervous system into blissful, obliterated goo.

Not once.

Not twice.

Okay, maybe three times, if we're being honest.

But semantics aren't the point here.

The point is—what the fuck happened to my hair?

I scramble toward the edge of the bed, grabbing

the gilded hand mirror that lives on the nightstand like it's going to save my life.

And what do I see?

Gray.

Okay, not really.

More like silver.

Freaking silver streaks. Like tinsel and glitter, but prettier.

Tons of them shimmer right through my previously all-dark, healthy, glossy-brown hair that I've always—*quietly, not obnoxiously*—loved.

I'm not especially vain. But come on. I had good hair! And now?

I'm rocking what looks like early-stage magical girl menopause.

"I mean it, Alaric," I snap, turning toward him. "What the hell is this?"

"Streaks of starlight, *Myrrin*. The mark of the Lords of the Eyrie. Now we match," he drawls from the bed like he's auditioning to be the cover model of *Fantasy Sultan Quarterly*.

One of those silk sheets is slung across his hips in a lazy V, but otherwise?

Seven full feet of smug, muscled, tattooed Demon Dragon Lord is on full, glorious display.

I hate how good he looks.

Like, viscerally.

It's not fair. I never look that good.

"And I disagree. You look fucking amazing," he adds with a grin that's pure sin, reclining back on his elbows like my minor existential crisis is foreplay.

I narrow my eyes. "Fine. Not gray hair. Silver streaks. But why? I mean, who authorized this?"

"Magic," he answers, completely unbothered. "The Eyrie. The Fates. Me. The zareth. Take your pick. You're mine now, and Nightfall doesn't want anyone to doubt it or to forget it. Well, something like that."

I throw a pillow at his head.

It bounces off harmlessly.

"Come back to bed," he says, extending a hand in that smooth, confident way of his.

Like sin with a side of smirk.

I frown at him. Amused, but trying not to show it.

"You look beautiful, Myrrin. I mean it. I like that we match now."

That gives me pause.

I glance at him again and—*huh?*

I hadn't noticed it before, but his raven-dark hair is streaked too. Threads of silver shimmer through it like moonlight cutting through shadow.

Ethereal and impossibly perfect.

The Fates didn't just mark me. They marked him too.

And not just his hair.

Now that I'm paying attention, I can see it—on the curve of his horns, in the subtle glow on his collarbone glyphs, and even along the edges of his wings, which I'm just now realizing he can tuck in and out of reality at will.

Which, okay, is kind of neat. Especially for bedroom antics. Because wings. You know, they can get in the way of things.

Of course, it all suits him.

Of course, he looks like some seductive, post-apocalyptic fairy king.

Meanwhile, I look like I lost a fight with a glitter bomb.

He crooks a finger at me. "Come. Back. To. Bed."

"Not until you explain why my hair looks like I got hexed by a glam rock witch."

He chuckles, deep and amused. "It's a mark of power. Of belonging. Of Fate." He lifts a brow. "And if it helps, I think you look like a goddess freshly fallen from the sky."

I try to hold my glare. I really do.

But he's all lean muscle and silver-shadow and sincerity, lounging half-covered in silk like some decadent prince of sin.

And I'm just me.

Slightly freaked out and also hopelessly, stupidly smitten.

"Fine," I mutter, crawling back under the covers. "But no more nookie. I don't want to wake up with a tattoo of your ass on my forehead."

Alaric chuckles low in his throat, already curling his massive frame around mine.

"Myrrin, I assure you, that will not happen."

I shouldn't love it when he cradles me close. But I do.

That velvet heat of his body pressed to mine?

It's addicting.

He makes a contented noise and wraps his arms around me.

I narrow my eyes.

"Alaric."

"Hmm?"

"No tattoos. Anywhere."

"Of course not."

A pause.

Then, far too casually, "Well, not yet. But I

admit, my Dragon sigil on your back? The tail snaking around your hip? Perhaps later."

"What?!"

He must see the weariness in my eyes, because he lifts the blanket and pats the space beside him with a crooked smile.

"Shhh. Sleep now," he murmurs, tugging me close. "You're safe, and you're mine."

And despite myself, I melt right into him.

Silver hair and all.

I mean, we've been tangled up for hours, and there's no clock in this room, or come to think of it, in this whole dang realm far as I've noticed.

I have no idea if it's even morning, but my body is starting to crash.

"Sleep," he whispers, voice a sinful purr in the shell of my ear, "Dream of all the wonders of us."

"But Alaric, I don't like needles—"

"No needles. Just sleep now. We'll talk tattoos and markings later, *my viyella.*"

And damn it, I do as he says.

I fall asleep in the arms of a Dragon.

Marked, claimed, confused as hell, and just a little in love.

Because who needs normal hair when you've got

silver strands of magic and a mate who holds you like you're the only treasure he's ever hoarded?

A warm breath stirs against the back of my neck.

My body aches—*in the good way*—and I'm snuggled against a literal wall of muscle and heat that is Alaric, who's currently spooning me like he owns the position.

Which, to be fair, he kind of does.

Or did, several times over.

I'm somewhere between dreams and reality, vaguely aware of how content I feel for the first time in what feels like years.

Until, suddenly, BANG.

CHAPTER 19
JULES

The door to our chamber flies open.

"Lord Alaric!" Shade's voice cuts through the room, urgent, sharp. "They've breached the North Road!"

"What the—" I jerk up, pulling the sheets with me, only to freeze when two enormous male figures loom in the doorway behind her like gods of war.

Alaric is already sitting up beside me, hair wild, tattoos glowing faintly like embers.

His voice is all gravel and fury when he growls, "Speak."

One of the men steps forward.

Broad, shirt unbuttoned, bronze-skinned with

curling black horns jutting from his temples, he answers in a voice made for battlefield speeches.

"They're attacking the villages at the base of Mount Thorn," he says grimly. "The SoulTakers. They've come in force."

Alaric snarls.

That sound reverberates straight through my spine.

The other man leans against the doorframe, nonchalant in a way that makes me nervous.

His eyes are pale. I can't tell the color. But his smile? It's sharp. And are those feathered wings? I blink.

"You sleep too long, Brother. I can see why, but it's a good thing we showed up before your borders burned."

I scramble to pull the blankets higher, realizing I'm still naked and very much on display for these two warlords or Demon dudes or whatever they are.

Alaric's eyes flick toward me, and with a flick of his wrist—*snap*—magic washes over me.

I feel refreshed, like I just took a shower. Even my teeth feel brushed and my breath is minty.

Silk wraps around my skin, soft and warm, forming into a deep midnight-colored dress with silver sparkles dancing across it like stars. It's belted at the waist with braided leather.

Practical, but beautiful.

My hair lifts from the pillow and falls into a quick twist, secured with a small silver pin shaped like a dragon in flight.

I blink, stunned, and whisper, "Uh, thanks."

"Kael. Dagan," Alaric bites out. "Don't pretend this caught only me unaware. The SoulTakers are getting bold. But my guard will be ready."

He doesn't look at me. Standing up, I see he is dressed in leather pants and what looks like an armored breastplate.

"Cozy. So, this is she? Your human?" one of them, Kael I think, asks.

Alaric snarls at the two men, though the other one is not even glancing my way.

"You will not look upon her," Alaric says coldly. "She is mine."

Kael snorts.

"We noticed. May I offer my congratulations, my lady? Oh, hush your snarling, Alaric. I'm simply surprised you claimed her so quickly. And I didn't expect Nightfall to mark her as well."

The other one—*Dagan, I think*—raises an eyebrow.

"You congratulate him when you accuse me of moving too fast for simply scouting out some locations in the Earth realm?"

Shade clears her throat loudly, stepping between me and the doorway.

"Lord Alaric, Lords Kael and Dagan only arrived moments ago. Their forces are gathered at the base of the Eyrie. The people are afraid. Some are here, at your door—"

Alaric snarls and rises from the bed.

Tall, powerful, bare.

I have one second to be crazily jealous, but Shade's gaze is averted, and he already had that same whip of magic dress him in leather and armor.

His wings are back, too. Dark and powerful, and I know I should be afraid, but I'm not.

When he is wearing his true Demon form, Alaric looks like a dark angel.

Like a Fairy King or some dark pirate.

Magic and strength seem to wrap around his body like the cloak of a warlord.

The glyphs on his skin are everywhere now, and seem to glow brighter as he stalks forward.

"*Myrrin,*" he says, turning to me. "You're safe here. Shade will stay with you."

"Wait, what's happening?" My voice cracks a

little, and I hate it. I hate the sound of my own fear, brittle and raw. "Who are they? What exactly do the SoulTakers want? Are people going to die? Are you walking right into danger?"

His expression flickers.

Just for a second.

But it's enough.

Anger. Regret. Worry. And something even deeper than that.

The need to protect.

It carves itself across his face before he pulls the mask back down, smoothing it into the composed, unreadable mask of the Lord of the Eyrie.

"I will not let them reach you," he says, and his voice is iron wrapped in velvet. "They want fear. They want dreams. Souls to fuel their dark power. And they will get neither from the Eyrie."

I push the covers off and swing my legs over the side of the bed, ignoring the fact that I'm still wearing this beautiful, but the gossamer-thin dress he conjured around me.

Lovely, but I'm usually a yoga pants and t-shirts kind of gal.

"I want to come with you. Maybe I can help."

I don't know how—shit, I don't know anything

except that the idea of him going out there alone makes my chest cave in.

"No, my viyella. You must remain in the keep."

He moves to a large armoire that hadn't even registered before.

It's made of some kind of dark wood and I wonder if it's sentient because it seems to open and close drawers before he touches it.

It's carved with shifting glyphs that seem to glow faintly when he gets close, and inside them are all manner of things.

He waves his hands, and the two largest doors open, and inside I see shelves of glass vials, pouches, polished stones, and blades that shimmer with quiet menace.

The scent of sandalwood, smoke, and steel fills the air as he selects a few items with terrifying precision.

Powders. Oils. Tiny bottles that crackle faintly with static.

He attaches them to the belt now wrapped around his waist, sheathing a pair of wicked-looking knives at his back and slipping a longer curved blade across his chest.

He's dressing for war.

And not just any war.

His kind of war.

One laced with magic and prophecy and death.

"But Alaric—" I step toward him.

He turns.

His pupils are slits now.

His eyes glow like molten silver under a full moon.

And the low rumble that echoes in his chest isn't just a warning. It's his Dragon, risen and ready to fight.

"Stay. Here."

The command lands heavy, like the whole room just dropped ten degrees.

My breath catches in my throat.

My body reacts before my mind can—*shoulders locking up, stomach twisting.*

Not because I'm afraid *of him.*

Because I'm afraid *for him.*

I nod once, swallowing hard.

But deep inside, I know I won't be able to sit here if something happens.

Because I love him.

Even if I'm not ready to say it.

Even if I'm not sure he's ready to hear it.

Even if this battle might be the one that proves what we are... or breaks us completely.

Then he turns away, his wings unfurling as he strides toward the door.

Kael glances back at me once, curious.

"Brave, this one. And clever, too. I like her."

Dagan snorts. "You would."

They vanish behind Alaric, and the room feels colder for it.

I sit back slowly, the silk of the conjured dress clinging to my skin, heart pounding with the knowledge that something big is happening.

Bigger than me.

Bigger than all of this.

"Shade," I whisper, stepping closer. "What will the SoulTakers do if they get past Alaric's guard?"

She pales at the mention of them. Her usual sparkle—gone. Her long red braid looks dull in the low light, and her hands twist together at her waist like she's trying to keep herself from shaking.

"I-I don't know. They're the monsters who don't ask permission, Lady Jules," she says softly.

Her voice is different now. Low, reverent, scared. "They take. They destroy. And now they're here."

The air shifts with the weight of her words.

Take.

Destroy.

God. That's what Alaric is facing right now.

And I'm standing here, wrapped in a silk shift, marked by this realm's magic like a prize, while the man who claimed me—*who I have irrevocably fallen for*—walks into something he might not come back from.

No.

No, I can't just stand here like a decoration in a fairytale tower.

I straighten my shoulders. "Will you help me find something else to wear?"

Shade looks surprised. "Something else?"

I nod once. "As much as I love the traditional garb of Nightfall, I can't just sit in a dress while Alaric is out there fighting a battle. I need to do something."

There's a beat of hesitation.

Then, softly, "Yes, Lady Jules."

She crosses the room quickly and presses her hand to a portion of the wall. A soft hum fills the air.

Stone shimmers, rippling like water, and a door appears that hadn't been there before.

"This is your closet," she says, stepping inside with a cautious glance. "You only have to think about what you need, and it will appear."

I follow her in.

And immediately stop.

Rows of gowns—*each one more exquisite than the last*—hang from gleaming silver rods that float a few feet above the ground.

The air smells like crushed petals and starlight, and every surface glows faintly with magic.

The shoes alone could fill an entire boutique.

I could stay here for hours.

But not now.

I walk deeper, scanning past shimmering ball-gowns and embroidered robes until I find what I'm looking for—*a section hung with clothing in deep tones, fitted pants, belted tunics, cloaks, and boots.*

Familiar. Practical.

The kind of gear I wore when riding Alaric's Dragon form.

"Lady Jules?" Shade asks nervously.

"These are perfect," I say firmly, and begin to get dressed, shedding the delicate silk dress and pulling on a pair of leather pants and a sturdy tunic cinched at the waist with a belt.

I spot a long coat—*lined in what looks like midnight velvet and clasped with silver*—and shrug it on, the weight of it grounding me.

Shade still fidgets in the doorway, wringing her hands. "Forgive me, Lady Jules, but a, a Lady of the keep doesn't usually—"

"I'm not really a traditional Lady of the keep, am I?" I say, tugging my boots on and turning to face her.

"Besides, I'm the *viyella* of the Lord of Air, Master of the Eyrie, keeper of Winds, and whatever else he told me he is," I say and grin, though my heart feels heavy. "To me that means the people who came here scared and looking for protection are mine to care for, too."

Her eyes widen.

"Now, bring me to where Lord Alaric's subjects are waiting. The injured, the frightened, the ones who've had to flee. And make sure we have food, clothes, anything else they might need."

She swallows hard. Then nods. "Yes, Lady Jules."

And I follow her—*through glowing corridors and echoing stairwells*—because if I can't be at Alaric's side wielding a sword, I can be here, ready to hold the line for those who can't.

I can be his strength behind the walls.

And if the SoulTakers think they've seen everything of the *Lord of Air's* power and might, well...
they haven't met me yet.

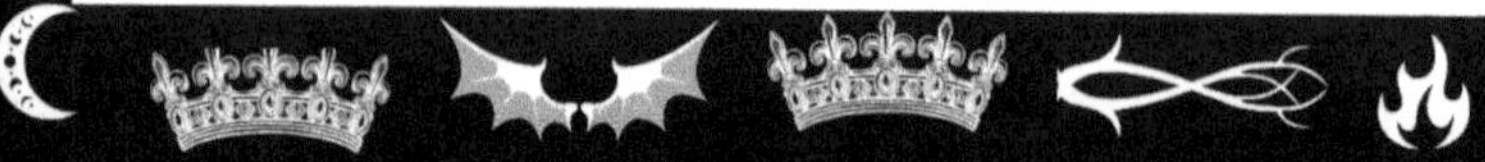

CHAPTER 20
ALARIC

Smoke curls through the sky like dark serpents, trailing from the pyres and shattered siege carts that litter the field.

The battle below thunders like an angry god.

Steel on steel, screams carried on the wind, and the unnatural growl of SoulTakers in their frenzied bloodlust.

Tents line the ridge behind our frontline, a makeshift war camp rising from the snow-dusted earth like a desperate gasp of order in a storm of chaos.

I have seen this before. But never have I felt so unsettled by it.

Because it's too close to her.

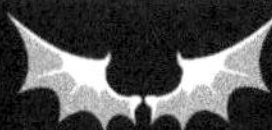

Because it is my fault she is here.

And if anything should happen?

I will never forgive myself, and the whole realm will suffer for it.

"How do they have so many?" Dagan growls as we duck into my command tent, brushing aside the heavy flap just as another distant explosion rattles the ground.

Blood and soot streak his jaw, and one of his curved axes still drips with black ichor.

"The SoulTakers have never been this organized," I admit grimly. "I was not expecting their numbers. Or their tactics."

"None of us were," Kael agrees, shaking off his helm and dropping it onto the nearest table.

He grabs a mug of mead and downs half of it before wiping his mouth.

"They have formation now. Rank discipline. Reinforced fronts. What the fuck is that about?"

"They've got a new leader," Thorne says, his voice like gravel as he enters behind us, black robes swirling and his fire magic already prickling against mine.

"A necromancer from my lands."

"From the Broken Plains?" Kael asks.

"Yes. He calls himself a Dark Sage. Master of the

Dead. But his name is Idris."

I snarl low in my throat.

"I know the name. He used to be a monk of the Silver Flame."

"Yes! He was until he burned the abbey to the ground and stole their relics," Dagan mutters, throwing a dagger onto the battle map with a loud thud.

"He's the one? Well, that explains how he's raising shadows, pulling from the very veil that keeps the death realm sealed."

I glance at the map. Lines mark our position on the crest of the Vale, just south of Mount Thorn, with our forces fortified along the two ridgelines bordering the North Road.

But we're stretched thin.

"Their dead don't stay dead," Kael mutters, scowling. "I watched three of my men take down a SoulTaker beast. And then it got back up."

"We'll hold them here. We must," I say.

My voice sounds calm. But inside?

I burn.

It's been seventy-two hours since I left the Eyrie.

I haven't slept.

I haven't shifted.

I haven't allowed myself to think about anything but the fight.

But I feel her.

My Myrrin.

My viyella.

Jules' emotions seep through our bond.

And they humble me.

Gods, I believe that woman might actually love me.

Me? Imagine that?

I don't deserve her or her love. Not with how I tricked her to begin with. But now that I have it? I plan to keep it and her.

Mine.

My Dragon agrees.

Her presence is a silver thread in my chest.

Tugging. Anchoring.

If I fail here—*if I fall*—those monsters will take her.

And the thought alone is enough to make my Dragon shake the fucking foundation of Nightfall.

"I've sent Dauphiné to the Eyrie," I say, forcing myself back to strategy, the battlefield map before us blurring at the edges of my vision.

Kael arches a dark brow. "I saw that. She came seeking sanctuary when her borderlands fell," he muses, sipping mead like we aren't half a breath from war.

"And did you warn your lady fair about your old love interest coming to stay?"

My jaw flexes. "I never had anything with Dauphiné. You know that."

"Does Jules? Does she know anything about the woman?" he counters.

I cut him a look sharp enough to cleave steel. "Shade will put her in the south wing and see to her needs as a guest of the Eyrie. That's all."

Dagan chuckles without humor. "Wait. Dauphiné? That noble bitch from the Onyx Marches? Thought she had you marked as hers once upon a time."

"She did, but I was not on board," I say tightly, the words scraping like stone in my throat. "No matter. I have a mate. Jules is all that concerns me. Dauphiné is an ally and a guest of the Eyrie. That is all."

A moment of silence stretches. Until Thorne speaks, calm and careless. "I thought Jules was a means to an end—"

I don't remember crossing the space between us.

But one second, I'm breathing through the hot pulse in my temple, and the next, my hand is around

Thorne's throat, slamming him back against the center pole of the war tent.

The entire space shudders with the force of my fury. His boots drag the dirt.

"She is my viyella," I snarl, voice low and lethal. "And you will give her the respect she deserves."

The fire in Thorne's eyes flares higher—*but it's not defiance. It's realization.*

"Truly, Alaric?" Dagan asks, slower now.

There's something in his tone. A shift.

I release Thorne. Step back. Look each of my brothers in the eye.

"Yes," I say, firm. "She is my fated mate. My viyella. And we share the zareth."

A weighted silence settles in the tent.

Thorne rubs his throat but bows his head.

"Apologies, Alaric. I did not know."

"None of us did," Kael mutters, his tone less amused now. "That kind of bond. I haven't seen a Lord share one with a mate in generations."

"It changes things," Dagan adds, arms crossed, golden eyes watchful.

"It changes me," I admit. "Everything I do now is for her."

A beat.

"Still," Thorne says, ever the strategist, voice

gravel-low. "Might be wise to watch Dauphiné. That woman's ambitions have teeth."

I nod once.

They're right to be wary.

But I'm no longer a Lord playing pieces on a board.

I'm a male with something to lose.

And that makes me dangerous.

I nod.

"I trust Shade to keep her out of trouble. My concern is here."

Kael refocuses on the map. "We'll need to collapse the northern trench and push our Archers to the south. If we can hold that long enough for Thorne's sorcerers to finish the ward circle, we might buy ourselves a breather."

"I'll take a flight patrol to harry their supply chain. Hit them hard and fast while they're distracted by the line," I add.

"And if Idris' shadow beasts reach the second tier?"

I slam my hand on the table. "Then I go Dragon. And I burn every fucking inch of their corruption off this mountain."

Silence answers me.

Then Dagan smirks.

"You always did have a flair for the dramatic."

"Nightfall doesn't need flair," I growl, already calling the air to my veins. "It needs fury."

And they're going to get it.

Because I am the Lord of Air.

And no one—*no one*—will harm what's mine.

CHAPTER 21
JULES

THE EYRIE

The last couple of days have gone by in a blur.

I miss Alaric like crazy.

But even more wild than that? I can feel him.

Not just memories or longing.

No. It's like he's *inside* me, stitched into every breath I take, a silver thread woven through my soul.

His concern.

His fury.

His sharp-edged focus.

It hums in my chest like a second heartbeat, echoing through the bond we share, and even though we're miles apart, it makes me feel closer to him.

I know what he's doing is dangerous. I know it's

vital. And I don't want him to worry about me while he's out there facing whatever horrors the Soul-Takers are throwing at him.

So at night, when exhaustion pulls me under, I lie in our bed—*his bed*—curled around one of his pillows with my hand resting over my heart. I focus on the warmth of our connection, and I send him everything I can muster.

Hope—because I am very hopeful for us and our future.

Love—because even though I haven't said it, I feel it. For him.

I send him reminders that I am here. Waiting. Watching for him.

And that I'm thinking of him.

That I'm longing for the day he comes back to me.

Meanwhile, I'm learning.

About Nightfall. About the Eyrie. About what it means to be Lady Jules, which is a title I'm still not fully sure I deserve.

But I can't get anyone to stop using it, so I might as well embrace it.

The Eyrie is huge—*like, Hogwarts-had-a-baby-with-an-elven-castle huge*—and I still get turned around in the corridors.

Shade says I'll get the hang of it. I say we need some of those *you-are-here maps* like they have at zoos and shopping malls.

There are attendants everywhere, kind and strange and quiet, and while I've met several of them, I admit I have a hard time keeping all their names straight.

They bow a lot. One of them offered me a tiny dragon fruit thing yesterday, and I wasn't sure if I was supposed to eat it or name it.

Harold, though—Harold I adore.

He's head of the kitchens and gives serious no-nonsense-grandpa energy.

He grumbled the first time I asked for something sweet and fizzy, but after I showed him how to make whipped milk foam and shape it into little hearts, I think he secretly fell in love with me. In a platonic, tea-sipping, grumble-while-stirring kind of way.

There's no coffee here—*tragic*—but they do have something close. The people call it fyrran, a dark, rich brew made from roasted sunfruit seeds, and honestly, it slaps.

There are also teas for everything.

Sleep, energy, stomachaches, lust—you name it.

Nyna, one of the cooks, even showed me a type of gelatin made from flower stems, and I used it to mold little fruit jellies in the shape of stars and moons.

The kids went nuts for them.

It helps, all of this.

The routine. The budding friendships. The quiet sense of belonging I feel when someone calls me Lady Jules without hesitation.

This place could be home—*feels like home*—even if a piece of me is still raw without Alaric beside me.

Right now, though, there's a ruckus coming from the kitchens, and that usually means something's on fire or Harold is yelling again.

I walk in, brushing flour from my palms onto the apron I'm wearing over a loose blouse and fitted pants.

Shade helped me modify the blouse, adding ties at the arms so I could roll them up without dragging them through whatever stew I'm stirring or bandage I'm tying.

We've had a steady stream of displaced families arriving from the lower villages—people whose homes were destroyed or made unsafe when the SoulTakers breached the North Road.

Some are nobles, but most are just scared families trying to get through another day.

Alaric's estate is massive, and while many are

staying in the outer houses around the Eyrie, we've made space inside for those who need more care.

The kids are my favorite.

Sticky-fingered, full of questions, and bold enough to ask me if I really did ride a Dragon or if Alaric just wears a costume for dramatic effect.

I assured them, quite seriously, that he does not do cosplay.

We've been doing arts and crafts in the play-room—*well, they make crafts, I mostly try not to get glue in my hair*—and I read to them in the evenings.

Shade found me a collection of old Nightfall stories, full of heroes and monsters and weird enchanted objects.

I swear one of the stories was about a pair of talking boots that fell in love—*isn't that amazing?*

Truth is, I've been *okay*, all things considered.

But when I walk into the kitchen and see Harold with a vein bulging in his temple, I know something's up.

"What's the matter?" I ask, wiping my hands on my apron as I step forward.

Harold throws up his hands in dramatic despair.

"That blasted woman again! I made her venison twice, and now she says the potatoes are '*too aggressive.*' What in the blazes does that even mean?"

"Lady Jules?" Nyna steps up beside me, her expression apologetic. "Um, apologies, we have a guest who is making some demands."

I already know who she means. I heard some of the attendants whispering about her.

Dauphiné.

They say she's a noblewoman. A guest of rank. An important ally of the Eyrie.

Respected. Honored. Needed.

And yet, I've heard the whispers.

The kind that slip under doors and echo across cold stone floors when servants think you're not listening.

The ones spoken behind half-closed doors with tight mouths and wary eyes.

They say Dauphiné once had her sights set on Alaric with the kind of focus that felt less like admiration and more like a hunt.

That her father—a powerful Northman from just beyond the Thorn Mountains—once tried to arrange a match between them. One that would've combined territories and strength.

But Alaric refused.

And according to the whispers, she didn't take it well.

They say she lost her mind.

Tore through her own home—something the attendants call the *Winter Court*, though none of them seem to say it fondly.

Apparently, the Eyrie is the only true seat of power in these parts, and she never quite got over that.

In fact, according to those pesky whispers, she still thinks there is hope for her.

She wants the crown.

She wants him.

And though he already denied her, she still covets Alaric.

Nyna told me how Dauphiné made her rage known.

Publicly. Violently.

Declaring herself the only one worthy of ruling beside the Lord of the Eyrie.

Of reigning not just over the North, but perhaps all of Nightfall.

Part of me—*the smaller, weaker part*—wants to shrink at the thought.

To question everything.

To let that old familiar ache of insecurity creep in, whispering that I don't belong here.

That I'm just a woman swept up in a fantasy.

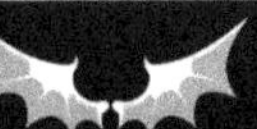

That this place, this power, this man—*it was all meant for someone else.*

But I won't.

I refuse to let jealousy or fear get the better of me.

Not when Alaric isn't here to speak for himself.

Not when I know in my heart that what we have is real.

That I am not some placeholder in his bed or a pawn in a political game.

I am his viyella.

And until he tells me otherwise, I'm going to act like it.

Which means taking care of the people under this roof, no matter how difficult—*or highborn*—they are.

And if Dauphiné is causing this much tension in the kitchen alone?

Then maybe it's time we met face to face.

Because I can't protect the Eyrie from behind a curtain.

And no one—*no one*—is going to walk all over the people I've come to care for.

Not even a beautiful—*I have to assume she is beautiful, I mean, most everyone here is*—bitter noblewoman with delusions of grandeur and a past with the man I love.

I exhale slowly, offering Harold a quick pat on the shoulder.

His grumbling has reached full teakettle status, and his face is red enough to match it.

"I'll handle it," I murmur.

His eyes widen. Harold clutches his apron and pats his face with it.

"Oh! Thank you. But are you sure, Lady Jules? She's been barking orders like she thinks she's Queen of the Realms. Tried to fire Nyna three times just this morning. I don't want you to go through any trouble for me."

"It's no trouble. And let her try that with me. I'll show her what it means to be a Jersey Girl," I grumble.

I don't even mean to sound so sharp. But I'm tired. I miss Alaric.

I haven't heard his voice in days, only felt his presence through the zareth.

I don't need some highborn drama queen making life hell for the people trying to hold this place together.

"Lady Jules, are you sure?" Nyna asks in a small, frightened voice.

"Yep. I'm sure," I mutter, tugging off my apron. "I think it's way past time, I have a little chat with our noble houseguest."

Because I might not be a queen or a general or a born Lady.

But according to Alaric and everyone else here, *I* am the Lady of the Eyrie.

This is my home.

And I'm done letting spoiled strangers treat it otherwise.

I arch a brow. "So, what are Dauphiné's latest demands?"

I ask, wanting to prepare myself.

Shade appears from the back corridor, her usually calm demeanor visibly fraying at the edges.

Her cheeks are flushed, and her braid is half undone, which says a lot.

"It's well, you see, Dauphiné is *unhappy* with her accommodations."

Nyna winces.

Harold grunts.

"Unhappy how?" I ask, already bracing myself.

"She says her suite is too dark, the silks are too coarse, the fruit is too ripe, and she's sent back four meals in the last day. She also keeps trying to enter Lord Alaric's private chambers."

I blink. "I'm sorry, she's doing *what*?"

Shade nods tightly. "She insists she must see him. Claims it's her right."

I narrow my eyes and take what's supposed to be a calming breath—but I must be doing it wrong because I feel anything but calm.

The moment she sees me, Dauphiné straightens, her pale violet eyes narrowing with interest—*and disdain*.

She's tall, willowy, stunning in a way that screams old money and even older magic. Her silver hair is twisted up in elaborate coils, glinting like ice under the glass ceiling of the sun-drenched room.

Her gown is pure drama, layered silks in shades of frost and midnight, clearly designed to intimidate.

Too bad I'm not in the mood to be intimidated.

"Who are you to deny me?" she demands, each syllable laced with venom. "This is Nightfall, not some tiny village of squabbling hens. I am Dauphiné of the North. My father once held many treaties here, and I *was* promised Alaric's side."

My steps are slow but steady as I close the distance between us.

I can feel Shade trailing just behind, nervous but resolute.

"Alaric isn't a prize to be promised," I say calmly, my voice sharp as broken glass.

"He's not a throne or a name to inherit. He's a person. A protector. And whether or not he ever intended to choose a consort, I can promise you one thing. He's not into women who throw tantrums over flowers."

Her nostrils flare. "You think you can speak for him?"

I lift my chin.

She's stunning.

True.

Way taller than I am, with midnight blue hair and cold silver eyes.

She is svelte, thin and fit, wearing a gown that would put everything and anything on Earth to shame.

Her clothing is rich, her posture perfect, her beauty the kind you expect from a fairytale. But her beauty is diminished by her expression.

But for all her beauty, she looks unhappy.

She looks like a woman who's been told her whole life she was owed the world.

Better than all. Beholden to none.

And it's soured her.

"I asked you a question. Just who are you to tell

me what I will or won't be getting?" she asks, her tone dripping with venom.

"We haven't been introduced yet because I've been attending to the victims of this battle. My name is Jules," I say calmly.

"Jules? Who do you think you are talking to me this way?" she asks, snorting a laugh at my expense.

"Lady Jules is the Lady of the Eyrie, Mistress Dauphiné. She is Lord Alaric's viyella, his *Zharaya*. His Dragon's true rider," Shade steps forward, bowing slightly and making the introduction.

I feel pride emanating from my first friend in Nightfall and I can't say it doesn't boost my confidence.

I lift my head, watching as Dauphiné's haughty glare turns black with rage.

"What? Impossible! This *person* cannot be his Zharaya!"

"It is quite possible, actually," I turn my head, ensuring she sees the bite mark Alaric gave me high on my neck.

"You will never be granted access to his chambers. Not since I'm the one in Alaric's bed. I'm the one wearing his mark."

Her nostrils flare.

"But you're human! Not of Nightfall! Your body

is too soft and fat! You are not a Demon! You are lowborn! You don't even have magic!" She screams.

"Yes," I say, stepping closer, refusing to flinch. "I am all those things and I'm also not going anywhere."

She looks at me like she's measuring me up for a fight.

"Enjoy your little romp while it lasts. But know this—power draws predators, Lady Jules. And when he's had his fill of you, you'll be discarded like the rest."

Shade lets out a shocked gasp behind me.

I smile sweetly.

"Thanks for the warning. But you're the guest here, Dauphiné. And while I won't throw you out completely—*because unlike some people I have manners*—I will have your belonging moved to one of the houses outside the Eyrie since you've managed to insult every single person in this household. You will be safe, fed, and housed, but I expect you to act like a decent person while you're under Lord Alaric's protection, or you can go find shelter elsewhere."

Dauphiné scoffs, but says nothing more for a moment.

"I don't have to. He marked me."

I don't shout it. I don't need to. The words hang in the air like thunder after a lightning strike.

Her eyes drop, flicking over my form, no doubt seeing the faint shimmer of silver in my hair. The same silver that now threads through Alaric's.

A hiss escapes her throat, low and furious. "Impossible. He would never—"

"But he did," I interrupt. "And even if you don't recognize the bond between us, Nightfall does. The Eyrie does. You're here under Alaric's protection, and that means you're under mine as well. You will be treated with dignity and fairness. But break one more thing, insult another servant, or try to lay claim to something or *someone* who is not yours," I step forward again, eyes locking with hers, steel behind my calm, "and I will have you escorted from the grounds. Sanctuary ends where sabotage begins. Am I clear?"

There's a long, charged silence.

"Shade," I say, without looking away from the angry noblewoman, "please make sure Lady Dauphiné's belongings are moved, and that she and her attendant have everything they need to feed themselves for the next few days," I say, then I meet Dauphine's glare. "And Shade? Make sure nothing from the Eyrie that she doesn't need goes with her."

The dripping of water from a broken flowerpot and the faint rustle of Shade's robes echoes in my ears. That, and my own heartbeat.

Dauphiné's lip curls, but she doesn't speak.

She simply turns her back and stalks to the far end of the solar, spine rigid with rage.

Shade lets out a breath she's clearly been holding.

"Lady Jules?"

"I'm fine," I say, though my heart is hammering.

"Let her sulk. She can enjoy her new accommodations and eat the food our people work hard to prepare. But she's not going anywhere near Alaric's chambers."

Shade gives me a look that is half awe, half terror. "I'll see to it, Lady Jules."

I nod, but I don't move right away.

My eyes linger on the shattered pot, on the beautiful flower that now lies crumpled on the floor.

A small gift, broken by someone who couldn't stand to see beauty that wasn't hers.

I crouch, brushing the dirt from the petals, and set it gently on a nearby table.

"Send someone to see if it can be saved," I murmur.

Because I know how it feels to be uprooted.

And I sure as hell know how to survive it.

Then I turn on my heel and walk out.

A thousand emotions bat at me, but I don't care to indulge in them right now.

I want Alaric to come back. To tell me that woman has no rights to him. To explain wholly what I am to him.

But right now, I have no choice but to go on. And no matter how long he is gone, this is still my place.

And I will protect it.

Until he tells me otherwise.

CHAPTER 22
ALARIC

THE RUINS OF THE FIRST BATTLE

The battlefield reeks of ash and blood.

The air pulses with dying magic as we drive the last of the SoulTakers into the dust.

My blade gleams red under the dying sun, my wings tucked as I shift back to skin and stalk toward the center of the chaos.

Behind me, Kael roars, his trident splitting the skull of a retreating monster.

Dagan is covered in ichor, his hammer slick with ruin.

Thorne, silent and deadly, turns a howling Demon to cinders with a flick of his wrist, his power is dark and biting like shadow made fire.

We've won.

Or so it seems.

It's been far too long since I've held my viyella and my skin itches with the need to go to her. My Dragon stirs, writhing beneath my skin.

Soon. We will be with her soon.

We've captured one of their generals. He is a massive creature, mutilated by his vows to Idris and his ilk.

This putrid smelling cretin is responsible for the deaths of many of my people. I growl as I draw near.

Even covered in blood and gore, cloaked in broken armor made of bones, with writhing tattoos pulsing beneath his gray flesh—*this motherfucker smiles at us.*

He's kneeling now, bound in runes, his eyes glinting with malice even as blood drips from his mouth.

"Speak," I demand, stepping forward, fire flaring in my palm.

"Where is your master? Where are the rest of your cursed kind hiding?"

The general laughs.

A sound like grinding glass.

"You think this matters?" he rasps.

"Doesn't it?" Thorne asks, pulling on the general's hair so he is forced to make eye contact.

"Tell us what you know or I swear by all the gods. I will smite you and all your wretched kind," Dagan snarls.

"This battle is just smoke and mirrors. You should appreciate that, Lord of Illusion," he says and laughs darkly.

"Speak clearly. Where is Idris? What is his endgame?"

"This fool will tell us nothing," Kael grunts, frustration showing as he slaps his hand on his leg.

"What is the matter little Lord? Maybe you've chosen the wrong side. Ally yourself with Idris the Great and you will know true power," he cajoles.

"True power, is it? Then tell us, General," I sneer, revulsion filling my voice, "why must he steal it from the souls and hearts of others?"

"You know nothing of power, lord of Hot Air and Trickery!"

"I ought to—"

"You can do nothing! You are *nothing*! This was but a curtain of smoke. A distraction."

My heart drops. A chill winds through my spine.

Dagan steps forward, snarling.

"A distraction from what?"

"The Eyrie," the creature hisses. "The Crown. We know where it lies. And your *pet human*? She'll scream loudest of all."

Everything stops.

The wind dies.

The ground feels suddenly unsteady beneath me.

"No," I whisper.

Then, *I feel it.*

A flash of terror.

Of pain.

Of wild, defiant fury, burning from across the bond like a lightning strike straight to my heart.

"*Myrrin*," I choke.

I can feel Jules through the zareth, as I have every night since I've been at battle.

But this time, she isn't sending me feelings of warmth, peace, and solace.

This time she's afraid.

She's scared, but she's fighting.

For the Eyrie. For me. For us.

They've reached her.

"What is it, Alaric?" Kael asks.

"They're storming the Eyrie! And I swear on every god imaginable, if she is hurt, there will be *nowhere* safe in Nightfall for Idris and his SoulTakers!"

The vow tears from my chest, primal and deadly. My roar ripples across the battlefield like a shockwave, shaking tents, flattening grass, and making even seasoned warriors flinch. The sky trembles in response. Magic answers me, thick in the air, crackling like a coming storm.

Without waiting for permission or another word, I swap skins.

My body *erupts* with heat.

Bones shatter and reform. Scales slice through skin as power roars to the surface. My wings unfurl with a deafening thunderclap, blotting out the moonlight. My horns spiral forward with a hiss of magic. My tail lashes behind me like a serpent made of obsidian.

I rise—massive, ancient, unstoppable.

I am Dragon.

I am Death to those who threaten what's mine.

Kael doesn't hesitate. "Go! We will follow!"

He plunges a dagger into the air, and his form dissolves into pure vapor, swept upward in a roaring gust of wind.

Thorne, Lord of Fire, becomes a living pyre. Smoke pours from his eyes as his body melts into

living ash, carried on currents only he can command.

Dagan slams his rune-carved hammer to the ground, and stone answers. Earth splits, surging up to carry him like a wave, the glowing sigils on his skin pulsing like a second heartbeat.

Together, we rise.

The Lords of Nightfall.

The realm *feels* us coming.

Winds scream. Trees bow. Magic bends and burns at our command.

The veil of reality begins to warp beneath our speed—space folding, time unraveling in streaks of silver and shadow.

Mountains blur.

Rivers vanish beneath us.

We *will* ourselves forward like divine weapons shot from the gods' own bowstring.

My wings tear through the sky.

And I feel her.

My viyella.

My mate.

My whole fucking heart.

The zareth burns inside me. It's an ache, a tether, a compass that leads only to her.

I feel her terror. Her courage. The battle in her

soul as she fights for the home we barely had time to build together.

"*Hold on, Jules,*" I growl, voice deep and echoing in the wind. "*I'm coming.*"

Nightfall itself splits open before us.

And the sky prepares to *burn.*

Then—*we're there.*

I can see the Eyrie, and it's under siege.

Fuck.

Screams echo through the valley as flames lick the lofty towers.

Smoke pours from shattered windows.

The great gates are splintered, and monsters swarm the halls I swore to protect.

But none of that stops me.

Because I see her.

My Myrrin. My sweet, furious, shining Jules.

She's a streak of motion on the marble steps—barefoot, blood-spattered, hair unbound and silver, catching the light like threads of starlight spun from war. A shield is clenched in one hand, her knuckles white, her eyes blazing with fire as she uses the other arm to usher a cluster of terrified children through the keep's inner gate.

Shade is at her back, staff whirling like a blade of moonlight, felling enemies twice her size with terri-

fying grace. They're both bloodied, battered, breathing hard.

But they are *still standing*.

And it *shatters* me.

A child screams. One of the SoulTakers lunges—more shadow than flesh—and Jules pivots with brutal efficiency, slamming her shield into its face with a crack of silver magic.

It drops with a howl, vanishing into a curl of black smoke, and she shouts something—*orders*—to the children, her voice fierce and commanding.

They run. They get to safety. And all because of her.

She doesn't see me.

Not yet.

My *Dragon* does.

And my heart—*our heart*—nearly breaks.

She's fighting alone.

For *me*.

For *us*.

She turns to face a new threat, blood on her cheek, teeth bared in defiance.

She is all instinct and light and raw, wild courage, and she has never looked more beautiful.

Never felt more mine.

I drop from the clouds in a streak of silver and rage.

My wings shatter the wind. My roar splits the heavens.

And then she sees me.

Her eyes lift. Find me. Widen.

Through our bond, I feel it—*relief.*

Hope.

That aching thread of welcome that binds soul to soul.

Take cover, I whisper through the zareth.

She doesn't argue.

Doesn't hesitate.

She *trusts* me.

I watch her grab Shade's arm, ducking behind the inner portico just as I *unleash fire.*

The courtyard *erupts.*

White-hot flame scorches the sky and silvers the stone.

The shrieks of SoulTakers echo, high and shrill, as they burn.

Their shadows disintegrate.

Their clawed limbs flail, trying to crawl away from my fury.

Too late.

My tail lashes through the air, smashing through the enemy ranks like a blade of molten iron.

Stone cracks beneath my claws. I tear through the courtyard like a storm, knocking down wave after wave.

I see faces I once knew—*Demons I once broke bread with*—now twisted by shadow, consumed by the madness of Idris's foul promises.

Gods help us.

This infection of SoulTakers, of power hungry madness, is *worse* than I feared.

Did the fall of our Prime truly send so many spiraling into desperation?

Has Nightfall forgotten what it means to fight for honor? For *hope?*

I don't have time for answers.

Not yet.

Because right now, my only thought—my only *purpose*—is to protect my *mate.*

Someone dares shout over the chaos. "*Kill the Dragon!*"

I twist toward the voice. A SoulTaker general stands atop the outer wall, blade raised.

Fool.

I rear back and *exhale* a blast of fury.

Flame roars from my throat—*pure silver edged*

with violet fury—and incinerates him where he stands.

It sweeps across the wall like a tidal wave of fire, obliterating the entire battalion at my gates.

Their screams are short.

Their punishment is eternal.

I land hard in the courtyard, stone shattering beneath me.

The last of the creatures scramble backward—but there's no escape.

I look up to see my brothers fighting for my homeland and I'm filled with a mix of pride and humility.

Thorne crashes down like a storm beside the eastern wall.

Dagan barrels through the gate, smashing everything in his path.

Kael flies overhead on glowing mists that look like rainbows in the light, hurling spears of lightning into the fray.

Then I turn, and I see her.

Right beside the doorway where *my viyella* waits for me.

I shift back in a blur, still steaming from the battle, and the moment I can, I grab her.

"Kiss me later," she snaps, breathless, eyes wild with adrenaline.

But I do it anyway.

I *kiss her* like the world is ending—because for a second, it almost did.

And then I press my forehead to hers, whispering the spell through gritted teeth, weaving ancient power into armor that blooms over her body.

Scales of my own dragon form, hard as myth, molded to fit her perfectly.

"You'll still be able to move. Still fight," I promise her.

She blinks, then looks down at herself. "Is this—"

"Magic, Myrrin. Armor of my own skin for protection. And this knife is enchanted as well."

I tuck the small blade into a sheath on her belt. I hate that she might have to use it, but it is there, should she need it.

"It's beautiful," she says eyes wide with wonder, and something else.

Fuck. She is so precious to me.

I cradle her face in one hand and my voice cracks as I gaze into her bright eyes.

"I'm sorry I took so long."

Jules lifts her chin, fierce and glowing and so fucking pretty my heart breaks just looking at her.

She lifts her hand, fingers brushing my cheek, and I lean into the touch.

"You're here now," she breathes, fierce and trembling, her hands tangling in my hair, splaying over my chest like she's anchoring herself to the only truth she can find. "And the people of the Eyrie need their Lord."

"No, Myrrin," I say, voice low and sure, though the ground still smolders with the echo of my rage. I press my forehead to hers, needing her closer, needing her alive, real, and with me.

Always with me.

"They need us. Both of us."

She blinks, and a smile blooms across her face—*soft and devastating, like the twin suns of the ancient stories, rising after the longest, darkest night.*

And in that smile, I see home.

I set out to steal a human, to use her as a pawn in a game as old as Nightfall itself.

I had plans, dark ones. Clever ones. Ones that were meant to cheat the Fates.

But the Fates—*fucking hell*—the Fates saw right through me.

They gave me Jules.

Not the compliant, docile creature I expected. Not a tool. Not a means to an end.

They gave me fire and tenderness. Wit and courage.

A woman who fights for others. Who holds children behind her shield and storms a solar to defend her place beside me. Who challenges me, holds me accountable, calls me hers without apology.

I am so fucking grateful it wrecks me.

So unworthy of her, it nearly brings me to my knees.

But gods help me, I will spend every breath proving I'm not a mistake she regrets.

I will earn her. Every day. Every night.

Because she's not just the woman Fate placed at my side.

She is the beating heart inside my chest.

More sacred than bloodlines. More valuable than magic. More real than any crown I've ever touched.

Jules is my whole heart.

And I will raze entire realms before I let the world take her from me.

"Then let's do this together."

Gods help me, I've never loved anyone more.

I raise my hands and call the spell.

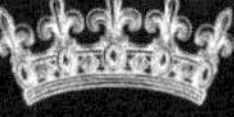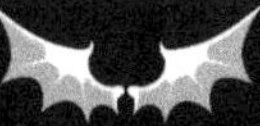

Magic races from my palms, imbuing even more threads of protecting into the shimmering Dragon-scale armor around her body.

It is lightweight, impenetrable, and made of *me*.

Fitted to her form so she can still move, still fight. But safer now.

Because she is not just *mine*.

She is *Nightfall's*.

And I'll burn the realms before I lose her.

CHAPTER 23
JULES

The Second SoulTaker Invasion At The Eyrie

For a moment there, it was touch and go.

I mean, I'm just a bartender from New Jersey.

I know how to pour a mean drink, charm a bad tipper into leaving a twenty, and talk someone out of picking a bar fight with a pool cue.

That was my world.

How was I supposed to know I'd be kidnapped by a seven-foot Dragon Lord with wings, eyes like molten fire, and a voice that makes my spine melt?

Claimed as his mate.

Pulled into the middle of a war between two ancient factions of a magic-wielding race from a realm that shouldn't even exist?

But it does exist.

And I've seen it now. I've *lived* it.

And the truth is, Nightfall means more to me now than I ever imagined.

More than I can explain without my voice breaking.

I've found something here.

Something that's more than just danger and magic and monsters in the dark.

I found him.

I'm in love for the first time in my life.

Real, soul-deep, fated-mate fairytale kind of love.

The kind that buries itself in your bones and whispers in your blood and makes you believe in impossible things.

And more than that—I feel *connected.*

To a place. To a people. To a role I didn't ask for but might have been born to fill.

Is that dumb? Naive? Hopeful?

Maybe.

But here's what I do know.

I won't be able to look myself in the eye if I don't stand beside him now.

If I don't fight for this place the way it's already fought for me.

If I don't give it everything I have—even if all I

have is grit and a half-decent right hook.

I'm not just Jules from Jersey anymore.

I'm viyella to a motherfucking Dragon. To the Lord of Air himself.

He is my *viyen*. He is my heartbeat. He is Alaric of Nightfall.

And I am his, wholly and completely.

So no, I'm not going anywhere.

I'm not running away and ducking for cover.

The fight is not over.

My place is beside Alaric. So, I stand right there, shoulder brushing his, breath still ragged from the chaos of battle.

Around us, smoke rises in twisting gray plumes.

The marble of the Eyrie's courtyard is scorched, smeared with ash and blood.

But we are not alone.

Alaric's brothers—Kael with his soaked tunic clinging to him, Dagan with his runes still glowing, Thorne burning with quiet fury—form a solid wall beside the Eyrie's remaining guards.

Together, we drive the last of the SoulTaker-corrupted soldiers into the open square at the heart of the Eyrie.

Our forces surround them.

Alaric's brethren, the castle guard, even a few

brave villagers still clutching farm tools and makeshift weapons.

United, bloodied, but unbowed.

The captured attackers stumble into a huddled group beneath the broken arches and scorched flags.

"Their eyes are vacant, unseeing," Kael murmurs.

He's right. They look like glassy like marbles reflecting a storm. Some snarl and spit like feral beasts, caught in a waking nightmare.

Others just weep. Silent tears streak down soot-smeared cheeks as they tremble, muttering words no one can understand.

"None of them seem aware of what they've done," Thorne agrees.

And I nod because he's right.

They don't seem to understand the havoc they've unleashed on this sacred place. Or the cries of the wounded, the blood that darkens the flag-stones beneath our feet.

Some stare at the bodies of their own kin lying among the fallen, and it's like they can't even see them.

But the others can. Even now, I can hear the weeping.

It cuts through the quiet aftermath like a blade

—mothers calling for children, lovers wailing over still forms.

Families who sought refuge behind our walls now crawl through rubble and ash to find the ones they couldn't protect.

Cloth is laid gently over lifeless bodies. Names whispered like prayers.

My heart cracks wide open.

I glance at Alaric, and even without meeting his eyes, I *feel* it—through our bond, pulsing low and steady in my chest.

This is wrecking him.

Every broken body. Every scream. Every reminder that the SoulTakers came here to wage war on the Eyrie. That Alaric's strength, though mighty, is not omnipotent and he cannot protect everyone.

He bears it like he bears everything else. Head high, spine straight, expression unreadable.

But I know him now.

And I can feel the storm behind the silence.

He aches for them.

So I reach deep inside myself and send him what strength I have. I don't know if it's enough, but I push it into the thread of silver light that connects us.

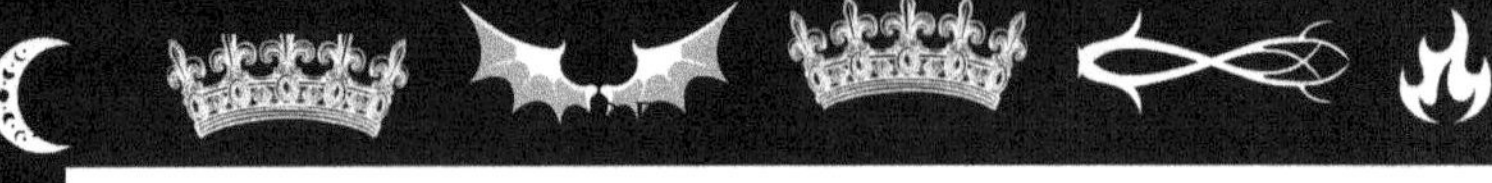

My love. My steadiness. My presence.

And I feel him catch it.

He doesn't falter, not even for a second, but I feel the way his breath hitches.

The way his soul curls around the gift like a man gripping a lifeline in a flood.

Thank you, the bond whispers back.

Emotion clutches my throat, and tears sting my eyes—not for me, but for him.

For all of us.

Because we are still standing.

And somehow, against impossible odds, we're still *together*. He squeezes my hand before stepping away.

"We must bind them," Alaric says to his brothers, his voice like thunder. "But do not harm them."

His magic surges forward, silver and furious.

The others follow suit. And I stand there breathless, as I watch them.

Earth, flame, water, and wind weaving together as glowing chains rise from the stone itself to wrap around the captured enemy forces.

I watch, wide-eyed, as some of the bound begin to sway and fall to their knees, confusion breaking over their faces like morning light through fog.

"What is this?" one mutters, blinking slowly. "Where am I?"

"They've been bespelled," Alaric says grimly. "This is SoulTaker magic. Twisted. Ancient. They've enslaved Demons to do their bidding. Not one of these is a true SoulTaker."

"It'll take time to free them all," Dagan adds, his voice low and angry. "This kind of magic runs deep."

"It will be a long night," Thorne grunts, kicking some scattered stones that sit at his feet in frustration.

It's weird, but I don't feel scared around these men—these Lords.

In fact, I feel like I'm standing with friends. Or big brothers.

Big, terrifying, ridiculously good looking, big brothers with elemental magical powers, who could level cities, sure.

But still, these guys? They feel like family.

They start with nods, a few hands pressed to chests, that kind of thing.

And just when I think it's all going to stay stoically respectful, Kael steps forward, all wet hair and ocean eyes, still bleeding calm and power from every pore.

"I just wanted to say thank you, my lady," he says in that low, rolling-tide voice of his.

"You fought like a warrior born. And you stood beside our brother, Alaric, when lesser women would have pissed themselves and begged for a portal home. You have my respect."

I blink. "That's, um, unexpectedly flattering."

Thorne—*of course*—snorts.

He's soot-streaked and smirking, leaning on a blade that looks like it melted halfway through the battle.

"I didn't think a mortal could hold her own against a SoulTaker horde," he drawls. "But you made me eat my words."

"You're welcome," I say sweetly, and he tips an imaginary hat.

Dagan's next. The quiet one. Hulking and stone-faced, with a rumble like distant thunder in his chest and a literal rune-glow pulsing along his arms.

He eyes me for a second like he's deciding whether to say something at all.

"We lost good people," he says finally, voice like gravel and grief. "But more would've died if not for you. You kept the children safe. You protected the Eyrie."

Then, shockingly, he bows low. "You have my oath."

I just stare at him. "Um. Thank you. That's— *wow*—that's a lot of oath."

"She's overwhelmed," Kael stage-whispers.

"She's earned it," Dagan counters.

Then one of the guards—*a young woman with a messy braid and a bandaged arm*—pops up, grinning sheepishly.

"My lady. You were terrifying. In a good way. Like a frenzy of weaponized energy. Also, you saved my brother, Thimble. He was one of the young you ushered inside."

I press a hand to my heart. "He's a sweet kid. But really, don't thank me. I just did what I had to."

"You also shattered a grown man's nose with a child's shield," Thorne adds helpfully.

"I didn't *mean* to do that," I mutter.

"But you *did*," Kael points out, grinning now. "And really, that was one hell of a shield bash. I saw it from across the courtyard."

"I thought I broke my hand at the time," I admit, laughing a little.

Cue Alaric, spinning toward me like I just announced I had a terminal condition.

He grabs my hand, turning it gently over and

inspecting every inch like it might crumble in his grasp.

"I'm fine," I tell him.

He doesn't believe me until he's pressed his forehead to mine and exhaled slowly like I just saved *his* life.

"For fuck's sake, Alaric," Thorne grumbles, "let the woman breathe before she bashes *your* head in."

"She's got good form," Dagan mutters.

Alaric growls under his breath, but I grin and kiss his nose before he can say anything dangerous.

He looks wrecked. And it's honestly unfair how hot he is when he's worried.

"Where did you learn to fight like that?" he murmurs.

"I didn't," I confess. "I sort of blacked out and let instinct take the wheel."

Thorne whistles.

"See? That's the good stuff. That's how most battles start. But not many end with the victor wearing Dragon-forged armor and swinging a kid's shield like a goddess of wrath."

"It was a *regular* shield," I insist, but it's drowned out by laughter.

Kael sobers just enough to bow his head.

"Doesn't matter what it was. You wielded it like you'd trained a thousand years."

Then Alaric's hand wraps around mine again—*warm, calloused, grounding.*

His thumb moves in a slow, reverent arc over my knuckles, and the simple touch steals the air from my lungs.

It's not just the way he touches me—*it's the meaning in it.*

The weight of everything he's saying without words.

And once again, I'm struck hard by how impossible he feels to me.

A Dragon Lord who shifts the skies with his will, and yet holds my hand like it's the most sacred thing in the world.

A man born of fire and legend, forged for war and leadership, yet here he is—*reaching for me like I'm the miracle.*

The ache in my chest blooms sharper.

Because somehow, in a realm where nothing makes sense, *he* does.

And that terrifies me more than any monster ever could.

CHAPTER 24
JULES

"She is fierce," he says, his voice low and reverent. "She is my viyella. And I thank the Fates every damn day they gave her to me."

The others go quiet, and I let the moment stretch, not quite able to speak. I never thought I'd feel like this.

Respected, seen, like I belong.

And finally, I admit the truth to myself.

Heaven help me.

But I wouldn't trade this wild, magical, chaotic life for anything.

And in that moment, I believe in Alaric. In his words. His truth.

I feel it.

Not just in the bond, but in the eyes of every person standing here. They don't see a human woman out of place.

They see one of their own.

And I'm just me.

Wearing awesome armor, my man magicked for me. But still covered in soot and sweat. Still shaking inside from the terror and adrenaline.

I don't feel like a warrior or a ruler. Just a girl who stumbled into a fight and didn't back down.

"I'm going to check on the children," I murmur to Alaric.

"If you wait, I'll come with you," he offers, brushing a strand of hair off my face.

But he's needed here.

"Don't worry," I murmur, pressing a kiss to his cheek, not because I have to, but because I *can*, and I *want to*. "I've got Shade with me."

Alaric's jaw tightens. He nods, but I feel the reluctance in every inch of him as his fingers trail down my arm before he lets me go.

My body aches, bruises blooming under my skin, but my heart—*gods, my heart is so full it might burst.*

"My lady? You wish to check on the children?"

Shade materializes at my side, quiet as a shadow, but her eyes are alert, bright.

I slip my hand into hers and give it a squeeze. "Are *you* okay?"

She tilts her head, a small smirk playing on her lips. "I am a Demon, Lady Jules. Battle sings in my veins."

And to be fair, she doesn't look shaken at all. Even streaked with soot and blood, with a bit of someone else's armor stuck in her braid, she radiates calm competence.

But she's smiling. And for that, I'm grateful.

I'm still reeling, to be honest.

I mean, no one tells you that when you're kidnapped to a new world, you'll end up in an actual battle for your life.

I wonder for a second if those tae kwon do classes I took in grammar school helped at all. Decide probably not.

What happened today? Well, that was all instinct. Fear. Protectiveness.

Still shaking slightly, I make my way into the keep with Shade while Alaric and his boys make a plan for detoxing those bespelled by the SoulTakers.

It seems like a long and heady process, but even as I leave his side, I know he will handle it.

We head toward where I sent the children during the battle—inside the Eyrie for their protection.

I feel a twinge of comfort at the thought of those precious tiny lives—Christol with his gap-toothed grin, little Allanah who always wants to braid my hair, and tiny Thimble who's obsessed with my Earth stories.

But the moment I open the doors and walk down the hall to the children's reading room, the one I had set up right outside the library, that comfort dies.

Dauphiné stands in the center of the room. Her terrible beauty seems even more unhinged than it was the last time we met.

Her hair is wild, eyes glowing unnaturally bright, a strange necklace with some kind of amulet glows strangely with something smoky and dark. She keeps clutching at the thing, hissing when she does.

The torn and frayed gown looks like it was once intended for a wedding. Not a war. And her emotions are everywhere, going from anger to fury to despair.

The Eyrie seems to pick up on them, and I swear it's like the keep is trying to calm her.

Rage drips from her voice like acid.

"You've ruined everything," she hisses.

Behind her, the children lie still, bound in shimmering coils of magic. It's like they've been drugged, or maybe magicked by some sleeping spell.

Above their tiny forms, daggers hang in midair, pointed down, trembling as if her magic might just drop them at any moment.

My heart stops.

"Mistress Dauphiné!" Shade gasps, skidding to a halt beside me as we burst into the quiet nursery chamber turned nightmare.

My heart drops.

The children—*Christol, Thimble, little Allanah, Anchor, and Beffany*—are slumped in a neat row on floor cushions, unmoving.

Suspended above their tiny, slumbering bodies are three blades, hovering midair, trembling slightly with magic.

At any moment, they could drop.

Dauphiné stands at the center of the room, arms raised like a conductor orchestrating death.

Her once-perfect gown is torn, her hair wild, eyes gleaming with feverish light.

"What are you doing?" I demand, stepping forward.

My voice is cold, sharp steel laced with fury. I can't help it.

How dare she do this?

"You might fool the Lords," she says, her voice curled in contempt, "trick them into thinking you're brave and strong. But I know better. You feel too much for those beneath you."

"Is that what this is about? You think kindness is weakness?" I ask, my tone clipped.

"Dauphiné, let the children go. Whatever this is, whatever delusion you're spiraling into, we can settle it between us."

"I would never sully my hands with you," she hisses. "A tavern wench from another world, dressed up in Dragon's silk. But he is the Lord of Illusion, right? Maybe you should take care what you choose to believe is true."

That hits in a way I didn't expect, but I push it aside for now.

"Look, whatever happened would you really harm children?" My voice rises, edged in horror and disbelief.

"Lady Jules," Shade whispers, and her horror is palpable. But I don't stay quiet, I simply can't.

"These are your people, too! How can you justify this?"

The woman's laugh is brittle. Cracked glass. And I know she's having some sort of breakdown.

"You fool. I would risk the entire North for what I deserve. Alaric was supposed to be mine! We were betrothed in all but name. I was raised to rule at his side, born to bear the next line of Lords!"

"No," I say softly, taking a step forward. "You weren't meant for him. If you were, he would've chosen you. But he didn't."

Dauphiné's face contorts, beautiful features twisted with fury and heartbreak.

"I loved him!" she shrieks, her voice fraying at the edges of sanity. "I waited. I endured. Year after year, I stood in silence, groomed like a prize mare by my father to one day stand at his side. And what did he do? He took lovers, meaningless consorts—while I rotted behind cold stone walls!"

"You were hurt," I acknowledge, my voice steady even as my pulse thunders. "But you can't force someone to want you. You just can't."

"He didn't have to love me!" she snaps, the words like broken glass. "He only had to choose me! That was always the plan! I was his. And Idris promised—he promised me—"

The name stills my breath. "Idris?" I echo, already dreading the answer.

"Oh yes," she hisses, eyes gleaming with manic triumph. "He came to me in dreams. Whispered sweet poison. Promised glory and vengeance and Alaric's heart on a platter. And I—I gave him everything. My will. My soul." Her hand flies to the locket at her throat, the cursed thing pulsing faintly with a sickly light. "My oath is bound to this locket. I let him in." The last words, she speaks them in a whisper that chills me.

"You—You're in league with Idris?" I breathe, cold horror settling in my bones.

"I almost had him," she spits. "I would have had him. Until you came. With your soft curves and your helpless little mortal eyes. He started to care for you. Gods, he *saw* you."

She's pacing now, steps erratic, breath ragged with hatred and something deeper.

Madness. Delusion. Both.

"I thought if I helped Idris—*if I betrayed the Eyrie just enough, revealed the cracks in Alaric's guard, let the SoulTakers bleed into the north*—then I could ride in as savior. Grant him my lands. He would owe me. He'd finally see what a queen I could be. He'd beg me to stand beside him. And together, we'd rule."

My heart twists. Not just for Alaric, not just for

me, but for what this woman was willing to become in the name of obsession.

"You're crazy," I whisper. "You talk about love, but everything you've done proves you never knew what love is. Alaric would die for his people. And you—" my voice cracks as I look at the sleeping children, innocent bodies lying inches from death, "you're threatening them to steal a crown that isn't yours."

Her eyes flash.

"He was mine!" she howls. "Until you came. A mortal. A nobody!"

Shade shifts behind me, silent and watchful.

Her fingers flex around her staff, ready. I nod once, just enough to signal her—*hold. Not yet.*

Dauphiné draws herself up, regal even now, though madness ripples beneath her skin like a second soul.

"If I cannot have Alaric," she snarls, "then I will have what power remains. I will have the crown. Fetch it, human. Or I will spill these brats' peasant blood all over *Lord Alaric's* beloved stones."

Her voice is low and serpentine, sticky with rage and venom. Over the children's heads, the blades tremble—*hovering*—waiting to fall.

And for the first time, I realize she's willing to do it.

I feel the zareth hum violently inside me.

And Alaric's terror flares across our bond like a thunderclap.

He's coming. But I may not have time to wait.

Not if I want to save them.

Dauphiné gestures, and the knives above the children tremble downward, glinting in the soft glow of the enchanted sconces.

My stomach flips, fury and fear roiling inside me like a storm.

I need to buy some time.

"You betrayed him," I say softly. "You showed the SoulTakers how to get past his guard, endangered the entire Eyrie, all to feed your obsession."

"I sacrificed for love!" she cries.

"No. You sacrificed for power. Love doesn't look like this."

The spell around the children shimmers.

Flickers.

Her control is slipping.

She's unraveling.

I just need a few more seconds.

"Shade," I say quietly. "You ready?"

Her eyes flash. "Always."

Dauphiné tilts her head, suspicion creasing her brow. "What are you—"

"Stalling," I whisper.

And then—I don't think.

I just move.

Because he would.

Alaric, with fire in his blood and thunder in his voice. He'd charge headfirst into danger to protect what's his.

What's sacred. What's right.

And those children on the floor? With their small, sleeping bodies and their lives balanced beneath glinting blades?

They're sacred to me now.

This place—*Nightfall*—isn't just a strange realm I was dragged into anymore.

It's my home.

These are my people.

And I will not let them bleed because someone like Dauphiné can't handle rejection.

I take a step forward. Then another.

She snarls something. I don't hear it.

Because all I can hear is the rush of blood in my ears, the hum of magic vibrating in my skin, the roaring in my chest that sounds an awful lot like my name in Alaric's voice.

Myrrin? What is it, my viyella?

The zareth pulses, and I know he can feel me. But he's too far.

I have to do this.

And I can do this because Alaric believes in me. He gives me strength. And now it's my turn to prove I deserve it.

My hand goes to my side where that small blade I was gifted from the battlefield rests, still warm from the forge-fire enchantment Alaric placed on it.

My fingers close around the hilt. My knees bend.

Shade is behind me, ready.

I don't need to look.

I feel her.

A shield at my back, fierce and sure.

This is it.

My heart is pounding, my muscles shaking, but my purpose has never been clearer.

I don't know if I'll survive this. If she'll strike before I can act. If the spell will snap and the blades will fall.

But I do know one thing.

I have to try.

Because I want to be the kind of woman who stands her ground.

Because I want to be worthy of the lord that chose me.

Because I want to be someone my mate can be proud of.

Because I refuse to let innocent children die.

And if this is how I go out?

Then I'll go out fighting.

For them. For him. For us.

CHAPTER 25
ALARIC

I am elbow-deep in magic, forging stone and steel from will and air, the ancient language of my blood echoing beneath my breath.

Sweat traces lines down my back, heat radiating from the effort of holding so many spells at once.

Beside me, Dagan and Kael shape the walls with precision and grim focus. This temporary structure —*part infirmary, part prison*—rises from the scorched earth like a scar we've etched into the aftermath.

Thorne stalks the perimeter, his fire magic flaring in warning as he reinforces the bindings on the SoulTakers' remnants.

I call them prisoners, but the word tastes bitter.

Many of these poor bastards were once our own. Bewitched, bespelled, broken in ways that make my stomach twist.

Gods. That they got this close?

That I didn't see it coming?

That this war touched her doorstep while I stood blind?

It enrages me.

These SoulTakers didn't just break through our defenses—they wore the faces of people we once trusted.

Warriors we fought beside. Neighbors. Friends. Beasts twisted by darkness, wielding magics not meant for this realm.

We cannot release them. Not yet. Maybe not ever.

But neither will I leave them to rot in pain. I owe them more than silence.

So we build.

We plan.

We bleed for order.

With a sweep of my arm, I summon the winds to carry word to the North, calling on alchemists, soul-healers, the last of the rune-callers hidden deep in the frost bound ridges.

We will need all of them if we're to save what's

left of the ones ensnared by the SoulTakers' black magic.

This—*this is penance.*

This is duty.

And still, it feels hollow.

The role of Lord has always demanded sacrifice, but lately I wonder if seeking the title of Prime is not ambition, but madness.

What good is a crown if it can't protect the heart it beats for?

Because now I have her.

Jules.

My Myrrin. My mate. My viyella.

And everything else dims in comparison.

I pause, just for a breath. Just long enough to feel it.

The mate bond—the zareth.

A sudden, crushing squeeze wraps around my chest—tight, visceral, unmistakable.

Pain.

Fear.

Terror.

Not mine. Hers.

"Alaric?" Kael's voice cuts through the noise, alert and sharp. "What is it?"

I turn, heart already thundering.

"It's Jules," I say, already moving. "Something's wrong."

And gods help anyone who stands in my way.

Pain lances through me—*sharp, hot, primal.*

My head jerks up, eyes wide.

Kael is at my side in an instant, his mist-dampened hand gripping my shoulder.

No more words.

I'm already moving, the zareth burning in my veins like a flare guiding me home.

I race through the shattered remnants of the keep's eastern archway, the halls echoing with the chaos still settling from battle.

Faster.

The bond pulls me like gravity, and I round the last corner just in time to see her.

Myrrin.

My whole heart.

She's standing in front of the children, brave and determined, but not armed for fighting whatever this sick magic is that is pulsating in the air.

My eyes widen. She is facing Dauphiné. And fuck, there is something wrong with her.

The noblewoman glows with sickening dark light.

Around Dauphiné's neck pulses a locket,

grotesque with power, veins of shadow crawling across her throat.

And then, before I can do anything, Jules moves.

She doesn't hesitate.

Doesn't falter.

She lunges forward—*beautiful, fierce, and so fucking breakable it guts me to see her like this*—and she plunges her blade into Dauphiné's cursed locket with a cry that shatters something inside me.

"No!" I roar, the sound tearing from my throat like a wounded beast.

I see it all—see what's happening before it fully unfolds.

The locket shrieks, magic fracturing outward, blood spilling from it like it's a living thing.

Blades hanging in the air above the children begin to tremble, to fall.

Jules moves, using her body to shield the children.

And I roar my fear and fury.

"Myrrin!"

A wall of wind answers my call as I scream her name, my hands carving ancient runes into the air, the breath of the North rising to obey.

"GO! NOW!" I bellow at the elements, the air exploding forward.

Steel is snatched mid-descent.

Blades deflected.

And time itself stutters just long enough.

I reach her as she collapses, her arms outstretched, cradling as much of the children's small, slumbering bodies beneath her own as she can.

Her blade lies shattered at her side.

The scent of blood and scorched magic hangs in the air like smoke after a fire.

I stopped the knives from hitting her.

All but one.

It fell too fast, too sharp—struck the edge of her armor and glanced off, slicing a thin red line along her jaw.

Just a scratch.

Just a breath of pain.

But it *shatters* something inside me.

My knees hit the stone beside her.

The world narrows to her heartbeat.

Her breath.

A smear of crimson streaks her skin, and I wipe it away with shaking fingers, my hand cradling the fragile strength of her face.

My palm trembles.

Thank the gods, she's breathing.

"Jules," I whisper, my voice cracked glass, all the fury and fear I've kept buried rising like floodwater.

Behind me, I hear the chaos still unraveling—Kael, Thorne, and Dagan tearing through the wreckage, dispelling what remains of Dauphiné's black enchantment.

Shade moves like a shadow at my side, her hands gentle as she leads the children away, each one waking slowly, confused and frightened but safe.

And all I can do is kneel here and hold her.

I kiss her cheek, her chin, her brow—*reverent, desperate.*

"Alaric?" she breathes, stirring faintly, lashes fluttering like wings.

Her voice is soft, bewildered. *Alive.*

"You foolish, fearless woman," I choke, wrapping her tighter against my chest, my body curling around hers like a shield. "You were supposed to *wait* for me. I told you I'd come."

She blinks up at me, dazed, her lips curving with quiet defiance.

"You're here now," she whispers, echoing the words she gave me earlier.

And just like that, I almost fall apart.

I almost unravel entirely.

Because I almost lost her. And I will never be whole again if I do.

I bury my face in her hair, breathing her in, shaking with too many things—*grief, gratitude, rage, and overwhelming love.*

"I'm here now," I vow, my voice raw and ragged.

"And I'm never leaving your side again. Not for anything. Not for crowns. Not for war. Not for the gods themselves."

She is my heart.

My viyella.

The fire in my blood and the calm in my storm.

And the only reason I still believe this realm—*this fractured, cursed place of war and loss*—is worth saving.

I clutch her tighter, needing the warmth of her skin, the rhythm of her breath, just to stay grounded.

"Tell me you won't leave me," I whisper against her temple. "Say you'll stay right here, where you belong. With me."

My voice breaks on the last words, the ache behind them too old, too deep, to fully name.

For a long moment, she doesn't speak.

She watches me with eyes like tempered silver— steady, unflinching, the gaze of a woman who's

walked through hellfire and stood tall on the other side.

And then, quietly, but with steel in her tone, she says,

"First, tell me the truth. About how you picked me. About why me, Alaric."

My throat constricts.

I know what she's asking.

And I know what I stand to lose if I get this wrong.

But I won't lie. Not to her. Not now.

So I loosen my grip, just enough to meet her gaze, and nod slowly.

"I won't insult you with silence," I say hoarsely. "You deserve all of it. Every arrogant, terrible inch of the truth."

She presses against me again, but this time, she's not retreating—she's anchoring me.

She places a hand over my chest, right where the zareth bond burns beneath my skin, and her fingers curl into the fabric of my tunic.

"That's all I want, Alaric. The truth."

I rise with her as she leans into me, standing on shaking legs. I hold her steady.

Because that's what we do now—*stand together*.

"Okay, Myrrin," I murmur, her name a vow. "I

will tell you it all. I will tell you everything. About us."

Her lips press together. Her eyes shimmer—*with tears, with power, with clarity.*

And in that breath between heartbeats, I know I would kneel before her, surrender every crown and every battlefield if she asked.

Because she isn't just my fated.

She is my redemption.

And she has every right to break me.

CHAPTER 26
JULES

Of all the things about Nightfall I don't understand—*the magic, the monsters, the endless politics*—the one that keeps gnawing at me, refusing to let go, is this one pesky little question.

Why me?

Seriously. Why did *he* pick me?

Why did Alaric—*this towering, terrifying, impossibly beautiful man who commands the wind and storms, turns into a mighty Dragon, and has the hearts of an entire people*—choose me out of billions?

Not just people on Earth, but across what I now know is a multiverse of realms?

What could he possibly see in me, a bartender

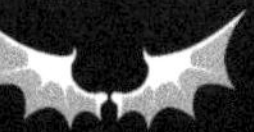

from Jersey who can barely make a latte without a sarcastic quip?

My body aches with every step as we walk down the long corridor toward the bedroom we share.

I'm bone-deep tired, bruised in places I didn't know could bruise.

And it's not just the battle that weighs me down.

It's everything Dauphiné said—*dripping with venom and jealousy, yes, but also with a bitter truth I can't quite ignore.*

That Alaric has taken consorts before.

That he's had lovers.

That maybe I'm just another passing infatuation until something better comes along.

I mean, yes, he claimed me, but what do I know about mate bonds? What if the magic gets old?

Will he grow bored with me once everything settles?

Once the novelty wears off and I'm no longer the strange, fascinating mortal with a smart mouth and a soft heart?

I don't *want* to think like that.

I *shouldn't* think like that.

But after the day we've had, the doubts sneak in like smoke under a locked door.

The children are safe now.

Shade made sure of it—she's already overseeing the families returning to their quarters while Kael, Dagan, and Thorne reinforce the wounded sections of the Eyrie and push the makeshift infirmary farther from the keep with their magic.

Alaric's decisions today have been swift and right. He is every inch the Lord.

But none of that matters now.

Not to me.

Because the war I'm worried about is the quiet one inside my heart.

When we enter the bedroom, I hesitate by the door.

I don't want to sit on the bed like this—in our battle gear, covered in soot and blood and magic residue. It feels wrong.

This moment between us needs something different. Something *real*.

And as if he senses that too, Alaric turns toward the fireplace, waves a hand, and two high-backed leather chairs appear, facing each other like we're about to negotiate a peace treaty.

Maybe we are.

He gestures for me to sit. I do.

And then he lowers himself across from me, his long frame taut with something I can't name—*guilt, fear, maybe even hope.*

"I will start from the beginning, *Myrrin*," he says softly, the firelight catching on the war-weary lines of his face, making him look almost mortal. Almost breakable.

"You deserve the whole truth."

I nod, but my stomach twists. Bracing myself feels useless when your world's already halfway shattered.

"You see, Nightfall has always had a Prime. A supreme ruler. A being chosen not just by bloodline or might, but by something older. Deeper. When one Prime falls, another must rise. That's how it has always been."

He pauses, and I watch his throat work, the truth clawing its way out.

"But the one chosen, well, it's never the strongest or the most ruthless," he continues. "It's the Lord with the clearest bond to his *viyella*. The one whose soul has been tempered by love."

My chest tightens so hard it hurts to breathe.

Of all the reasons I thought I'd been pulled into this madness, *that* one never crossed my mind.

"That's why the search began," he says. "Not for

warriors. Not for queens. But for mates. For the one bond that would ignite power strong enough to stabilize the realm. A bond formed not by strategy or convenience, but by something undeniable."

"And you found me," I whisper. My voice sounds far away, like it's coming from someone else.

Someone naïve.

He nods once, slow and agonized.

"At first, I thought—fuck, I was so arrogant. Foolish. Stupid. I thought I could trick the Fates."

The words hit like stones. Still, I let him speak.

"I told my brothers my plan. We all agreed, in the beginning," he admits, shame creeping into every word.

"We would find human women. Women from the Earth realm. See, we create dreams here, *Myrrin*, and the women of Earth? They dream the loudest and all for one thing above all," he says.

"For love," I whisper.

"That's right. We picked Earth because that's where women with the softest hearts are born. I just didn't know you also had the fiercest spirits."

It's a compliment.

But I don't feel any joy at his words, and sensing that, he continues.

"We believed we could find suitable potential

mates there. Charm them, seduce them into bonding with us. The magic would recognize the connection, whether it was real or not. Or so we thought."

"You *used* me," I murmur, a crack forming right down the middle of my heart.

He flinches like I struck him.

"No," he says quickly, shaking his head. "I *thought* to use you. That part is true. I thought I could simply choose a woman who wouldn't really *get* to me. One I could sway with illusion and pretty words. A means to an end. But then, when I got to Earth and began my search, I saw *you*."

His voice trembles now, low and hoarse.

"Instantly, I was drawn to you."

"Why?" I ask, not bothering to wipe my eyes.

"Are you serious? Do you not even know how beautiful you are?"

"I'm not," I say, shaking my head.

"I won't argue your beauty when it is simply fact, *Myrrin*. You weren't what I expected," he continues. "You weren't *any* of what I expected."

"So, pretty or not, you just picked someone you thought wouldn't matter."

The bitterness in my voice makes me flinch. But

not more than the hollowness blooming behind my ribs.

"I was wrong," he says, voice breaking. "So fucking wrong."

He presses a hand to his chest as though his heart is physically tearing inside him.

"I told myself I'd go through the motions—forge the bond, claim the power, and walk away untouched. Keep the lie alive. Maintain control." His voice is low, rough with emotion.

"But the second you stepped into my life, everything unraveled."

He swallows hard, eyes locked on mine, burning like twin embers in the shadows.

"Jules, I love y—"

"Don't." I flinch, the word sharp in the air between us. "You're just reacting. To the battle, to what happened. To relief. That's not love. It's adrenaline and guilt and pride all tangled up together."

"No." His voice breaks on that one syllable, fierce and full of truth.

"I knew long before today. Long before I saw you standing in the ruins like a goddess of fury, guarding children with blood on your cheek and fire in your eyes. I knew it when you made me laugh like a man, not a monster. When you challenged me without fear. When I realized, I didn't want to let you go."

I don't want to hear this. Because if it's real, I might give him all of me. And if it's not, I won't survive the crash.

"But you said it yourself, you're not supposed to love me," I whisper, voice cracking.

"I'm not supposed to feel anything. I'm the Lord of Air, my duty is to this realm. But you, you ruined all of that. I love you more than my name, more than my title, more than any claim I ever had on Nightfall. And gods help me, it terrifies me."

I try to steel myself, to laugh it off.

"Ha. I scare you? The mighty Dragon Lord trembling before one mortal woman?"

He smiles then, dark and raw and shaking with the weight of too much feeling. "Scare me? No, Jules, you terrify me. You wreck me. You make me forget how to breathe. You look at me and I'm not in control of myself. Don't you get it? You own me. You're my everything. My salvation. And I don't know how to survive that kind of mercy."

Silence pulses between us.

And for once, I'm not afraid of the quiet.

Because his voice is shaking.

Because my heart is pounding.

And because despite everything, I think I still want him to keep going.

I *can't* ignore what he's saying.

Because his voice is the sound of ruin and truth all at once, and I'm a woman already half-consumed.

CHAPTER 27
JULES

Sitting here with Alaric—*his knees brushing mine, the light casting shadows across his too-beautiful face*—I ask him to tell me the truth about us. About *everything*.

And it's the hardest, worst, most wonderful thing I've ever done.

In this world or any other.

Because part of me doesn't want to know.

Not really.

Not if the truth cuts deep enough to bleed out all the fragile hope I've been holding onto.

But the other part—*the fierce, stubborn part that has loved him from the moment he roared my name across a burning sky*—needs to hear it.

That part needs to know if I was chosen or just

convenient. Needs to believe that whatever brought us together wasn't just fate playing games.

So I sit still, aching and raw, braced for heart-break, breath held between the lines of what he *hasn't* said yet.

My heart is a storm.

My soul's already his.

And when he opens his mouth to speak, I'm terrified.

But I'm also ready. Because if we're going to burn, then let it be together.

Please.

"Nothing I could have planned would have ever prepared me for the wonderful reality of you, Jules."

I frown, caught between confusion and the soft, aching pull in my chest. "What are you talking about?"

He exhales, and something raw glimmers in his silver eyes.

"I'm talking about *you*. Your sass, your fire. The way you challenged me when others cowered. You never bowed. You *never* let the crown blind you. You saw *me—not the monster, not just the Dragon, not the Lord of Illusion with too much blood on his hands—but me*. And hell yes, you terrified me."

His voice breaks for half a second, like the

weight of it all might crush him if he doesn't get it out.

"Because when I claimed you, when I sank into your softness, your strength, your incomparable beauty—the truth is, you *claimed* me right back. You didn't even know it, did you? But you *have* me, Myrrin. Body, heart, and soul of a Dragon. The zareth doesn't lie. And I will never lie to you, by will or omission ever again. Even my Dragon chooses you. My Zharaya. Dragon Rider."

"But—"

"Shade told me you know what that means. Don't deny what we have, I beg you. I swear, from that very first time, our bond settled around me like fire and silk, and it didn't feel like power or strategy or seduction. It felt like *home*."

My throat burns. My heart's barely beating right. But I force the question, anyway, needing it like air.

"And the others? Dauphiné said—"

He doesn't flinch. Doesn't try to look away or sugarcoat the answer.

"If you want to hear about my past—*about meaningless nights and cold dalliances made in haste to satisfy a physical need*—I'll tell you. Every single one. If you insist. But those that came before?"

His jaw tightens.

"They were shadows, Jules. Flickers of hunger and nothing more. They never touched what you touch. They never saw what you see."

I swallow hard. "So they didn't matter, but I'm supposed to believe that I do."

It's not a question. It's a wound.

And Alaric steps into it like he's already bleeding too.

He cups my face, reverent and shaking.

"You *are* the only one who has ever mattered. And, for fuck's sake, Jules, damn me to hell if you must, but I swear, you are the only one who ever will."

His chest rumbles. His voice cracks. And the very air around him shimmers with magic.

"You do matter. You matter the most. Myrrin, you are *everything*," he swears. "Not because of what I was trying to do, tricking the Fates, which I obviously failed at because our bond is real. And not because the realm chose you. But because *I* did. Because the moment I stopped trying to fake my destiny, you *became* it."

The silence between us is thick with heat, heartbreak, and all the things we haven't said yet.

I shiver, cold for some reason, and a moment later a fireplace appears, roaring to life.

I smile softly and watch as it crackles and warms me to the bone.

The bond hums between us, not just magical—but raw, *real*.

And I don't know what tomorrow brings, or whether Nightfall will ever be safe again.

But this man, this Demon, this *Lord*—he is mine. And I think I'm his.

If I can forgive him.

If I can get past the how and why of it.

"I need to know you're not just enchanted by the idea of this bond," I whisper. "That if it faded tomorrow, you'd still want me."

He leans forward, bracing his forearms on his knees, his voice low and rough.

"The bond exists because of us, Jules. It isn't separate, but even if all of magic blinked out of existence, I would still chase you across a thousand realms to earn your heart again. You are not a convenience. You are not a tool for me to gain power. You are my viyella. My one true mate. I swear to you with *everything* I am, that is the truth."

I let that sit for a moment.

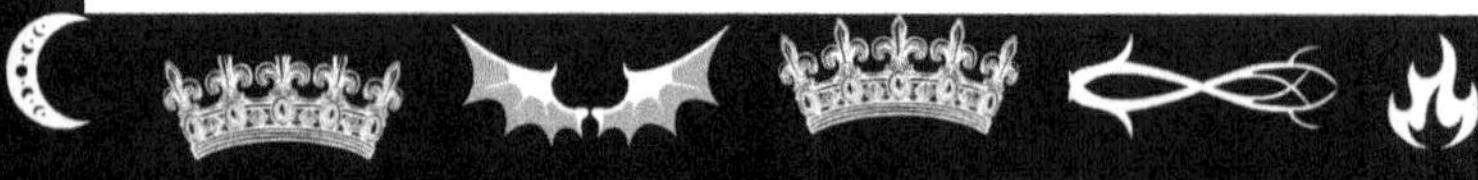

Then I speak.

"And you won't get tired of me? Won't someday decide the bartender with too many opinions isn't worth the trouble?"

His jaw tightens.

"Never. You are *mine*, Jules. Not because of fate. Not because of prophecy. Or arrogance. But because I love you." A pause.

"I am in love with you, Jules Strano. You are my one true *viyella*. Only you."

He says it so simply.

So devastatingly.

I forget how to breathe.

"Did you hear me, Myrrin? I love you," he repeats. "More than crowns, more than glory. If this realm asked me to choose between saving it or saving you—gods forgive me, I'd choose you."

And that's when I know.

The darkness here is real.

The danger is endless.

But this man? This Demon Dragon Lord?

He's the light I never saw coming. A storm wrapped in flame and shadow, and yet somehow, he's become my anchor.

My home.

And I'll fight for him. For this fragile, terrifying, exhilarating thing between us. For *us.*

Because I love him, too.

And loving someone like this? With your whole soul cracking wide open, trembling in its rawness? It means taking risks. Letting go. Bleeding if you have to.

For Alaric? I'll risk it all.

A hundred times over, I'd throw myself into the fire for him, and I'd still come out reaching for him.

"Jules," he murmurs, voice thick with worry and need. "Please. Tell me what you're thinking."

I lean in, eyes locked on his, heart pounding as I let my body do the answering.

"I'm thinking now would be a really good time for you to wave those magic fingers of yours and clean us both up."

He blinks, stunned. "What? Why would you—"

His breath catches as I slide from my seat and straddle his lap, loving the feel of his powerful thighs beneath me, fitting myself against him like I was made for it.

Because I believe I was.

"Oh, *fuck,*" he groans, hands going immediately to my hips, possessive and shaking.

"I want my *viyen*," I whisper against his lips, "to *claim* me again. Right here. Right now."

Something primal flashes in his eyes. That Dragon hunger I've come to crave.

A dark growl rumbles up from his chest and I feel it through every inch of me.

"For you, *viyella*?" he rasps, voice like sin and silk. "Anything."

Power crackles around us, seductive and sharp.

His magic washes over us in a heated wave— *slick and sensual, like the caress of warm silk.*

It strips away the grime, the blood, the lingering chill of battle with wicked precision, leaving us bare in every sense of the word. Body and soul.

And heaven help me, I don't think I'll ever get used to the sight of him like this.

Alaric looks like some divine creation—sculpted from shadow and starlight, his body carved in angles and muscle, power rippling beneath skin kissed by flame and magic.

Every inch of him speaks of battle, of command, of a life lived at the edge of a blade.

And yet, right now, he's not just a terrifying Lord of Nightfall.

Not just a beast who breathes fire and bends the wind.

He's just mine.

I let my eyes roam shamelessly.

The ridges of his abdomen.

The delicious V of his hips.

The long lines of strength and heat and the heavy, hard promise of what waits between his thighs.

My breath stutters in my chest just looking at him, and I swear, I feel my heart swell to match the ache building low in my belly.

But then I notice something.

He's looking at me the same way.

Like I'm the miracle. Like I'm the one who defies logic and fate and all things divine. Like I'm *beautiful.*

How can that be?

On Earth, I was nobody special.

Just another chubby woman with calloused hands and laugh lines, who poured drinks and smiled through the ache of wanting more.

There were prettier girls. Louder ones. Ones who knew how to get the spotlight.

But here, with *him*, I'm seen.

Desired.

Worshipped.

And the way he's looking at me now?

Like I'm some precious, irreplaceable treasure he still can't believe is his?

It nearly undoes me.

"Why do you look at me like that?" I whisper, voice trembling.

His hand cups my cheek, reverent, his thumb brushing the curve of my jaw.

"Because I never imagined in all my plotting and illusion building that I would ever find a creature as lovely as you and that you, in all your rare honesty and beauty, would choose *me.* You honor me, *viyella.*"

His touch follows, reverent and rough as his hands slide under the armor he conjured me, peeling it away like wrapping from a gift he's been dying to open.

"Alaric," I whimper, feeling needy and lost without him.

And because he knows it, he cups my hips and drags me closer, pressing his ready cock against my slippery seam.

We both groan. But he doesn't enter me. Just slides me up and down, coating his thick sex with my juices.

"I thought I nearly lost you today," he breathes,

his mouth trailing along my neck, my collarbone, his hands cupping me like I might vanish.

"You didn't," I whisper, tilting my face to his. "I'm right here. Safe. In your arms. And I *want* you so badly, *viyen*."

His grip tightens, restraint unraveling thread by thread. "You don't get it. I want you all the time. I need you, viyella. Have to *mark* you. Inside and out. I need every piece of you screaming my name, telling the world who you belong to, so no one—*not the Fates, not the gods, not any fucking traitor*—can ever take you from me."

My body responds before my mind can catch up —helpless against the force of his words, the way he says them like a vow, like a spell cast just for me.

Heat blooms beneath my skin, rushing in waves across my chest, my belly, lower.

My breasts grow heavy, nipples tightening as if summoned by the gravel in his voice.

Between my thighs, I throb, a new wetness flooding me in a sudden, shamefully eager pulse.

I ache.

Fuck, how I ache for him.

For his mouth, his hands, his body pinning mine down while he ruins me in the best possible way.

My skin tingles, hypersensitive, my breath

catching in my throat as every nerve screams for his touch.

The possessiveness in his tone—*the hunger*—it lights something reckless inside me.

Because I want to be taken.

Claimed.

Marked.

And never, *ever* let go.

"Then stop talking, Dragon Lord," I whisper, lips brushing his. "And fuck me already."

And thank fuck, he does.

First, he claims my mouth—*savage and starved.*

There's no patience in his kiss, no pretense.

Just teeth, tongue, and aching need.

He devours me with an urgency that leaves me gasping for breath when he finally pulls back, his silver eyes gleaming like wildfire.

I don't get a second to recover before I feel it —*him*—the thick, hard press of his cock grinding against the slick heat between my thighs.

My body bows toward him, every nerve ending lit up like fire in a thunderstorm.

"So hot and wet for me, *viyella,*" he growls, voice like velvet dragged over flame.

Then, with supernatural speed and strength, he

lifts me, spins me, and settles me on his lap, facing away from him.

"Alaric?" I manage, my voice breathless, unsure if I'm trembling from anticipation or the aftershocks of everything we've endured.

"I've got you, Myrrin," he murmurs, voice a promise etched in steel. "I *will never* let you fall. Just trust me."

And I do trust him. Yes, I really do.

One powerful hand braces my hips as he guides me down onto him.

I cry out, a sharp, shocked sound as he fills me—deep and claiming with one hard thrust of his incredible hips.

My fingers scrabble for purchase on his thighs, and he holds me steady, groaning low and filthy against my back.

"*Gods,*" I breathe.

The stretch. The heat. The way he pushes inside me—it borders on unbearable.

And still, I want more.

Alaric thrusts up hard, and my head falls back with a gasp, pleasure crashing through me in waves.

Then his hand slides around my waist, fingers seeking the place that drives me wild. When he finds my clit, he doesn't tease.

He plays me like an instrument he's mastered a thousand times over.

"Look at you, Myrrin. Wrapped around me like you were forged to take me. Do you even realize how perfect you are?"

"Alaric, more," I beg, and he never makes me wait.

He thrusts deeper, harder, making me see stars.

"You drive me mad, Jules. Every sound you make, every time you gasp my name—I live for it. I *burn* for it."

God, his words. They hit me hard.

Like adding fuel to the fire burning inside me. For him. Only him.

"Yes, only me. I want you ruined for anyone else. I want you aching for days because I claimed you too hard. I want my name to be the only thing your body remembers."

My body is so primed. So ready. I am seconds from exploding. And all I can think is how is it this good?

How is it possible it keeps getting better?

"Because I love you. And it will. Every time, Jules," he growls into my neck, "it'll be better. Deeper. Stronger. You and me, we were made for this. *For each other.*"

His words, his touch, the frantic pounding of our bond—*it breaks me wide open.*

I lose myself in the rhythm of our bodies. In the sound of our breath. In the heat of his hands and the low, wicked things he whispers in my ear between kisses.

"Don't think," he commands, voice low and rough, his teeth grazing the shell of my ear like a brand. "Just *feel.*"

And oh my God—I *do.*

I feel him.

All of him.

The dark, divine rush of his magic slipping over my skin like smoke and silk.

The weight of his body beneath me, heavy and anchoring, pressing me into the moment.

The raw possession in his touch, his thrusts, the way he holds nothing back, not even his heart.

I feel the way he loves me—*wildly, completely, without hesitation or end.*

"I love you, *viyen*," I gasp, the words torn from me as pleasure claws through my body, relentless and consuming.

His moves stutter. His chest heaves. Then he starts again, and pleasure feels like an all-consuming wave surrounding me.

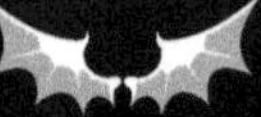

I'm floating on it. Soaring high above. Hovering on the edge of oblivion.

"*Fuck*, that's it," he growls, voice cracking on a groan as he slams into me one final time. "Give it to me. Mine."

And then we fall—*together*—dragged under by the storm we created. My body clenches around him, and I feel him thicken, pulse, and finally break with me, our cries lost in the magic that erupts like lightning around us.

The *zareth* surges, that sacred tether between us igniting silver and fierce, curling around our souls like a promise.

Our bond hums in the air, in our skin, in the shadows of the room. It lives.

"I love you, *Myrrin*," he whispers hoarsely, his lips brushing against the crown of my head as I slump back against him, utterly undone.

"I love you, too," I breathe, unable to do anything else.

His massive chest rises beneath me, rumbling with a deep, wordless sound that might be a laugh or a cry—*maybe both.*

And I just melt.

No more pretending.

No more wondering if I'm enough.

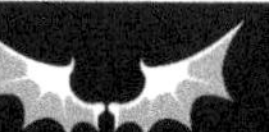

Because this man—*this miracle*—holds me like I'm everything.

I close my eyes, and for the first time in my life, I know what it feels like to be safe.

To be chosen.

To be *loved*. Not in pieces or conditions, but wholly.

And it's better than I ever dared to dream.

EPILOGUE ONE

JULES

 outside the Eyrie

Since there's still so much I don't know about Nightfall—*its history, its magic, its people*—I've found a way to begin learning that feels right.

Teaching the children.

Every morning, we gather in the newly built public library, a sunlit stone hall filled with scrolls and storybooks, with thick rugs for sitting, and shelves stacked with lore.

Alaric had it constructed just outside the keep after I offhandedly mentioned how nice it would be to have a space for the little ones to learn and dream.

I didn't expect him to follow through so quickly —*or so extravagantly.*

But he always does.

Fulfills my every whim as if it were sacred.

"As I always will, *Myrrin*," he murmurs now from the shadows, his voice low and warm with promise.

The moment he speaks, the class erupts.

A flurry of cheers, giggles, shy waves, and one bold little boy—*Thimble*—who throws his arms in the air and shouts, "Lord Alaric!"

I smile as my Dragon Lord steps fully into view, silver eyes softening when they meet mine.

And just like that, the day feels brighter.

He moves to lift Thimble up, giving the boy a spin before setting him down on his feet. Then he stands at my side without hesitation, his hand finding the small of my back like it belongs there.

Like I belong.

And I do.

Not just beside him—*but with him.*

As Lady of the Eyrie.

As his *viyella.*

And maybe—*please oh please*—something more.

Because the past few days have brought more than just peace to our lands.

They've brought stillness to my body, a deep

warmth blooming in my belly that no amount of magic can explain away.

I haven't told him yet—*haven't spoken the possibility aloud*—but every time I catch him watching me with that quiet reverence in his eyes, I wonder if he already knows.

Our bond has made us more than lovers.

More than mates.

It's made us readers of each other's souls.

His pride pulses through the *zareth* now, a comforting thrum against my skin as I lean into his side.

The children settle quickly, eager for today's legend.

Today, we're reading *The Three Stones of Seryth*, a Nightfall tale about a lost prince, the woman he falls in love with, and the magic they forge between them.

I wonder if Alaric chose it on purpose.

He often does things like that—*tiny, hidden gestures only I notice.*

It makes me fall harder.

Each day, I love him more. Not just because of the way he looks at me like I'm his whole sky, or the way he listens even when I ramble, or how he makes love like it's a vow.

But because of this life we're building.

Where he gives me room to grow,

Where I want to grow.

I glance over at him as the children open their scrolls, their little fingers tracing painted moons and golden ink.

Alaric meets my gaze and smiles.

And it takes everything in me not to blurt it out.

I think I'm pregnant.

Instead, I place a hand low over my belly and let myself simply feel the moment.

The joy. The hope. The wild, impossible beauty of it all.

Tomorrow, maybe.

Tomorrow, I'll tell him.

"Your thoughts are loud, Myrrin," Alaric murmurs, voice low and thick with meaning as the children begin to gather their things at the end of the lesson.

He motions for Shade to take over the reading of the tale as he walks me into the hall for some privacy.

His hand remains at the small of my back, grounding me. Anchoring me.

"I will call my personal physician to the Eyrie tonight," he says, silver eyes gleaming with pride.

My breath catches.

"You know?" I whisper, blinking up at him as tears threaten to well in my eyes.

He turns to face me fully then, the din of little voices falling away like mist as his silver gaze searches mine. His expression is reverent, almost stunned with joy.

"Of course I know," he says, brushing a knuckle gently along my cheek. "Your soul speaks to mine, viyella. Every beat of your heart echoes in my chest. And so does theirs."

I gasp, my eyes widening.

"Theirs?"

His smile turns soft and wild all at once.

"Yes, love. Dragons often have multiples. They are perfect. *Our young*. A presence unlike anything I've felt before. So new. So pure. And impossibly bright."

He presses his forehead to mine, his voice trembling now with awe and adoration.

"You have made me so very happy, you wonderful creature. You've given me more than I ever dreamed I could have."

Tears fall freely now, and I don't bother to stop them. They're not born of fear or uncertainty anymore.

They're born of joy. *Of love.*

"I love you," I whisper.

The words aren't nearly enough for everything I feel, but they're the best I have to offer.

He pulls me into his arms then, wrapping me in warmth and magic and the kind of unshakable certainty that I never thought I'd know. Not here. Not in this strange, dangerous, beautiful place.

But I do.

With him.

"I love you, too," Alaric breathes, kissing my temple with such fierce tenderness I swear I feel it echo in my bones.

"And I will love our young with every breath I take. As I love you, *Myrrin.* Until the stars themselves go dark."

And, in that moment, I know—with more certainty than I've ever known anything before— that there is nowhere in this multiverse I would rather be. Not Earth. Not some version of the life I used to think I wanted. Just here.

With him.

"You are right where you belong," Alaric says, his voice like velvet over steel. "In Nightfall. With me."

A laugh slips past my lips, soft but real. "Well,

technically, I'm only here because you came to Earth and stole me."

His eyes gleam with heat and something even more dangerous—*devotion*.

"And I'd do it again, *Myrrin*. Every. Single. Time."

He says it without shame. Without hesitation.

Like stealing me from everything I knew was the best decision he's ever made.

And maybe it was.

Because it brought me here—*to love, to purpose, to this impossible, beautiful life.*

To us.

To a love that makes my heart soar and my soul sing.

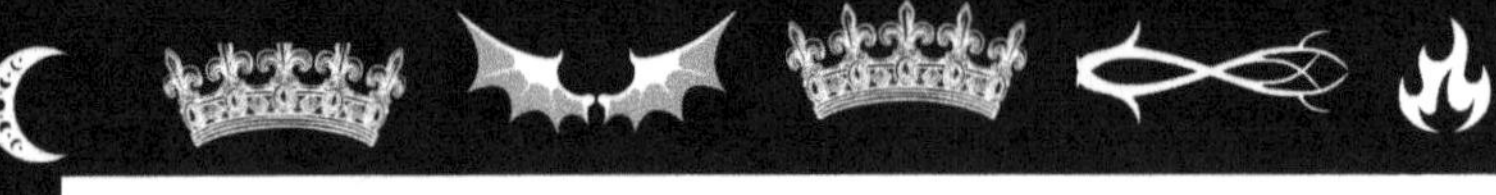

EPILOGUE TWO

ALARIC

The Eyrie to Castletide—the fortress of Kael, Lord of Water

After, when her soft cries have quieted, and she's trembling in my arms with satisfaction and sleep, I do not move.

I cannot.

Jules—*my Myrrin, my viyella,* my *zharaya*—is draped across my chest like she belongs there.

Because she does.

Her scent, wild and familiar, is laced with the heady truth that we are no longer just two souls bound by magic and choice.

We are more. A true family now.

The healer confirmed what my own instincts, and the zareth already whispered to me.

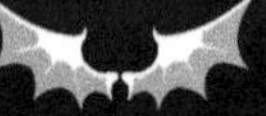
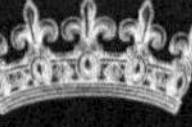

My mate carries our young.

Twins born of Dragon and heart, of shadow and hope.

Of love I never believed I was worthy of until her.

I press a reverent kiss to her forehead and feel her smile in her sleep.

Gods, she's radiant.

Fierce and soft. Flame and stone. Mortal and magic.

The ache I feel looking at her is so vast I don't know how to hold it all inside. I want to fight every enemy, burn every realm, and silence every whisper that might suggest she does not belong.

That she is not everything.

That she is not meant to rule beside me.

That our young are anything but miracles.

Screw them all.

Jules is the best thing that ever happened to me and I will spend eternity proving it to her.

And to that, that means I must make sure she is safe. Protected. Always.

Carefully, I slide from beneath her and pull the silk sheets over her bare skin.

She murmurs my name but doesn't wake.

I move to the center of the chamber and raise my palms.

With words in the old tongue, I call forth the sacred wards—the same ones carved into the stone of The Eyrie centuries ago by the first Lords of Nightfall.

Sigils of protection and permanence. Of belonging. Of bloodline.

My silver fire licks the corners of the room as the magic seals into place, shimmering silver and red and gold.

No harm will touch her here.

Not while I breathe. Not while I burn.

When I'm finished, I return to our bed, gathering her close again.

Her head finds its home in the curve of my throat.

And I let myself breathe.

One day, our young will ask about this moment. About their mother. About the realm we rebuilt together.

And I will say this.

It began with a storm, a stolen human, and a plan to cheat the Fates.

But what I found instead was something I never expected. It was tremendous.

Love.

Fire.

Everything I never knew was possible for me.

And I would choose her again. I would choose them again.

Every single time.

And now it's my duty to ensure Nightfall is ready to receive the gift of my children.

That it is the haven it once was.

I kiss her head once more, "I shall return soon, *Myrrin*."

The room dims as the wards lock into place.

My breath slows beside Jules' steady one, and for a single heartbeat, I allow myself to imagine a quiet life.

Then, I rise.

I do not wake her.

My viyella needs rest.

She has fought for this realm and suffered for it.

And now, she carries our future in her womb.

That sacred knowledge alone makes me want to stay. But duty calls.

Always, there is duty.

I call to the magic in my blood, and the Eyrie shifts beneath me.

Winds answer.

Stone sings.

The zareth pulsing beneath my skin coils

outward and bends space itself. My wings extend, bracing for the magic that will soon whisk me away.

And it does.

In the blink of a breath, I vanish—*traveling through ley-lines, through flame, through stone and time itself*—until I arrive at the cliffs of Castletide, Lord Kael's keep.

The air is heavy with salt and storm.

Waves crash far below, and the ocean pulses with ancient power.

Kael, Dagan, and Thorne wait for me in the watchtower, their silhouettes lit by the violet light of the fading moon.

I step forward, my boots echoing off wet stone.

"Do you have it?" Kael asks, his voice low, grim.

"I have the crown," I reply, reaching into the folds of my cloak and pulling the relic free.

Ancient, obsidian-black and etched with silver veins that pulse faintly with old magic.

"I figured this place was safest. They've already tracked it to the Eyrie once."

Thorne's mouth twists. "So you're finished hiding it? Are you saying you don't want it, don't want the throne anymore?"

I look down at the crown and my heart squeezes—for the fallen Prime who bore it last, and

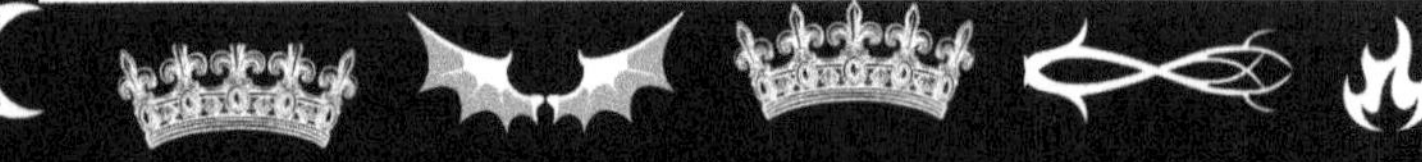

for everything we lost since the SoulTakers returned.

"I'll wear it, if I must," I say. "But Nightfall is not the only thing that matters to me now."

"Ah," Thorne drawls, that wicked grin curling across his smoke-smeared face. "You mean your *human mate*. I suppose the great illusionist himself couldn't keep up the ruse forever, eh?"

His voice is teasing, but there's a flicker of something else in it. Something brittle, vulnerable even.

I don't rise to the bait.

"No illusion is strong enough to outwit the Fates," I say, my voice sharper than steel, my stance unshakable.

"And I don't just mean my viyella. I mean my *family*."

That word lands like a spell.

The room goes silent.

Dagan bows his head. "Lord Alaric," he murmurs with quiet reverence, his earth-dark gaze filled with something rare—*hope.*

Kael's gaze sharpens, his ocean-colored eyes narrowing, the air around him stilling like the hush before a storm.

"No," he breathes, slow and stunned. "It can't be. Is it truly possible?"

I nod, the pride in me fierce and grounding, like the pulse of the zareth itself. "It is. Jules is expecting."

A pause.

"Twins."

The silence that follows isn't empty—*it's thick with shock, wonder, and something that tastes almost like awe.*

Even Thorne, usually quick with a crude joke or jaded laugh, goes still.

I press my palm over my chest. Over where I feel them—my mate, my children.

My whole precious world.

"I will protect them," I say, not a promise but a vow. "With every breath I draw. Nightfall may call for a Prime. But I—I have something more important now. I have her. I have them. I will not lose either to ambition or war."

"You've changed," Dagan rumbles, a flicker of emotion warming his granite voice. "You speak with the weight of a man who finally understands what it is to live for something."

Kael nods, quiet and thoughtful. "We all must change, I think. If we're to survive what's coming."

"And it's coming," I say. "Don't think for a moment that Idris or the SoulTakers are finished with us. They've tasted our blood. They'll come back for more. Stronger. Smarter."

"Then let us meet them with everything we've got," Thorne says. "And if that means finding mates, maybe not like yours—*not a real mate*—then so be it. I say we stay the course."

"You mean to follow the path I set? But I was wrong!" I ask, a flicker of dread stirring inside me.

"Don't get self-important," Thorne scoffs. "You got lucky. We're just trying to improve our odds."

"Luck," I repeat under my breath, though I know what I have with Jules is anything but.

Dagan folds his arms, his gaze steady.

"You may have found your heart, brother, but the rest of us still need strength. If the zareth bond is our best weapon, we'd be fools not to seek it."

Kael adds, "We're not chasing love—we're seeking survival. If finding mates on Earth offers us power strong enough to challenge Idris and restore balance to Nightfall, then we will continue. With or without your approval."

Thorne shrugs. "And let's be honest, you're just nervous one of us might be worthy of the crown, too."

That makes my magic rise, unbidden. A low growl rumbles through my chest.

"I told you. The crown doesn't matter to me anymore. My family does."

"Enough," Kael says firmly, cutting through the tension like a blade. "We are not enemies. We want the same thing. Peace. Strength. A future. Let's not tear each other apart while trying to save our world."

I breathe deep, then nod once.

"Very well. But tread carefully. The Fates don't look kindly on those who try to manipulate them. I nearly lost everything before I found what mattered."

"And now that you have," Dagan says, "you'll fight harder than ever to keep it."

I meet their gazes one by one. "Yes. I will."

And the oath that follows isn't just mine.

It's all of ours. A silent pact forged in blood, brotherhood, and the terrifying, sacred power of love.

Thorne steps forward, eyes gleaming like flame. "Then we stand ready."

I look at each of them—*my brothers by blood and bond*—and I feel it.

A shift.

Not just in the magic, or the air, or the realm itself.

But in us.

In what we fight for now.

The crown is no longer just a symbol of rule. It is a promise.

To protect. To rise. To lead with more than power.

To lead with love.

I set the crown down on the stone altar of Castletide, its jagged edges catching the sea-silver light that spills in through the high arched windows.

The weight of it is real. Heavy with legacy, soaked in sacrifice.

One by one, we each place our wards upon it—*ancient seals of water, flame, earth, and air.*

Magic hums through the chamber, the crown locking beneath our protection, hidden from those who would seek its power for ruin.

When the last spark fades, I turn away.

Let it rest. Let it wait.

My feelings now? The crown can go to another with my blessings.

Because right now, in this breath, in this heart-beat—*I have something far more precious to protect.*

"May your good fortune hold, Alaric," Kael says,

his tone quieter than usual, the sea in his voice calm, but watching.

"Thank you, brother." I pause at the threshold and glance back. "And please—consider my words. Trying to find a mate with a lie on your lips isn't as easy as you'd think."

Kael huffs a breath that might be laughter, or regret. "Maybe not. But for some of us, it's worth a shot."

I could argue. Could warn him again about trying to fool the Fates.

But what's the use?

Some truths must be lived to be learned.

Instead, I offer him a small nod—*equal parts warning and well-wish*—and step into the portal's shimmer.

The pull of the zareth guides me home like a lodestone to its true north.

And gods help me, I'm already aching for her.

For Jules.

My heart, my viyella.

My mate who fought beside me, burned for me, saved my people, and then looked me in the eye and loved me in spite or because of it all.

She is my reason.

And now, she carries my legacy.

I feel the flicker of it even before I step through the veil—*the thrum of two tiny heartbeats woven into the bond between us.*

Twins. Ours.

The next breath I take is the first in a new life.

A life I will guard with fang and flame and every ounce of the Dragon Lord I am.

Because for the first time in all the ages of Nightfall, I am no longer alone.

I am loved.

And I am home.

EPILOGUE THREE

KAEL

THE AIR HERE TASTES FLAT, HEAVY WITH SALT AND manmade chemicals.

Still, I breathe it in.

The veil between worlds thins near water—it's how I slipped through. Cloaked by magic and shadow, I move unseen, though this realm grates against my skin like sandpaper on wet stone.

Earth is ugly in the wrong places. Loud. Polluted.

But here? Here, at this so-called aquarium, something ancient stirs.

She stands knee deep in a pool, a curved smile on her lips, her hair tucked up beneath a cap, skin kissed by sun.

Curvy, golden, and radiant.

My fingers twitch.

"Good girl," she croons to the beast beside her—a sea lion, I believe they call it.

The creature barks, then nuzzles her hip like a pup.

She laughs, low and musical, and something cracks open in my chest.

Phoebe.

That's the name I stole from a badge near the edge of her station.

And though I knew nothing else about her, I knew she was mine.

Not just because of her beauty. Not because she speaks with the voice of kindness to creatures lesser men would torment.

It's deeper.

The tide shifted when I stepped near her.

My runes pulsed, burning hot beneath my skin.

The sea inside me—*what magic remains*—answered something in her.

She has no idea she's calling to me.

No idea that her soul might be the one the Fates carved out of foam and starlight to balance mine.

No idea what her touch could restore.

The sea has chosen her. And so have I.

I catch my reflection in the thick glass of the enclosure—horns curved back like black coral, runes glowing along my throat and chest like bioluminescent tide lines.

No glamour tonight.

No illusion.

Because the woman meant for me will see all of me. She'll have to.

I will not take her with lies.

But I will take her.

One moment, she's laughing at a sea lion's antics.

The next, the water around her begins to stir, curling unnaturally with currents that answer to me and me alone.

She gasps and turns—wide eyes locking onto mine as I step out of the shadows and into the light of her world.

"You—you can't be back here!" she says, but her voice shakes.

Not with fear.

With knowing.

With instinct.

I smile. "No, I suppose I shouldn't be."

Her breath hitches. The wind stutters. The sea hushes.

"But I came anyway. Because you called me. And now, Phoebe of Earth, I'm calling you back."

She stumbles as the water rises, swirling around her legs. My magic coils and leaps, a whirlpool blooming beneath her feet.

"No—wait!" she shouts, but the portal is already opening.

I reach for her as her world breaks apart, and mine prepares to welcome her home.

"What are you doing?"

"I'm taking what's mine."

To Castletide.

To my ruined lands.

To Nightfall.

THE END.

GLOSSARY

Fyrran – A dark, rich brew made from roasted sunfruit seeds. Strong and slightly bitter, it's the favored morning drink across Nightfall—most closely resembles coffee in the human realm.

Demons – The native people of Nightfall. Though referred to as "Demons," they are not evil, merely misunderstood by human myths. Humanoid in form, they possess varying degrees of primal magic and ancient bloodlines.

Karessa – A tender term of endearment meaning *"little flame,"* used between bonded mates or lovers.

Nightfall – A hidden realm layered just beyond the human veil. One of many planes in the vast magical multiverse, Nightfall is steeped in ancient laws and primal magic. Once ruled by a mighty

Prime, the realm now teeters on the edge of ruin after a brutal siege by the SoulTakers—interdimensional entities that feed on dreams, magic, and desire. The future of Nightfall hinges on those brave enough to claim love, power, and fate itself.

Myrrin – An affectionate word meaning *"my sweet."* Often spoken between bonded pairs to express closeness and emotional vulnerability.

Oona – A gentle endearment meaning *"seedling,"* symbolizing something precious and just beginning to bloom. Commonly used by protective partners.

Telya – Meaning *"pull of the tide,"* this phrase is most often used in the Tidal Lands to express deep emotional gravity—when a bond is as irresistible and inescapable as the sea itself.

Viyella (feminine) / Viyen (masculine) – A *fated mate.* A soul-deep bond decreed by the realm and the Fates. Rare, sacred, and unbreakable, the viyella/viyen connection forms the core of power for many of Nightfall's rulers.

Zareth – An ancient Nightfall word for the *soulbond* that binds mates not only through love, but through shared destiny, blood magic, and the will of the realm. When a zareth forms, power surges between the pair, often enhancing magical abilities and intensifying their emotional and physical connection.

Zharaya (feminine) / Zharan (masculine) – *Dragon Rider.* A true mate of a Dragon Lord, bound by zareth. The term marks one as chosen by both dragon and destiny, capable of enduring the fierce love and raw magic of a bonded Dragon.

EXCERPT FROM WEREWOLF FEVER

Books had always been the single most important thing to Mabel Ann. Why shouldn't they be?

Life in the smallest Pack in the western United States, having broken affiliation with the Macconwood Pack a hundred or so odd years ago, was hardly a hot spot for any other activity. Save fighting and fucking.

Mabel Ann abhorred violence and at twenty-six was still a virgin. For a Werewolf, she was certainly an odd duck. Probably had to do with the fact that while most she-Wolves were long and lean, Mabel Ann was a whopping five foot three and had more than few bonus pounds left over from her childhood.

Too old for it to be baby fat, she was, to put it

simply, a plus size Wolf with a *honky tonk badonkadonk* that may very well have been the inspiration for the song of the same name.

She stepped outside the small library she ran for the Zapata Pack and was grateful it was winter. Though too short for her liking, it was cooler and drier than the rest of the year in the southwestern Texas town where she and the Pack made their homes.

Her cell phone buzzed in her pocketbook, but she was on chapter thirteen of this really steamy paranormal romance from one of her favorite authors, and it was just about to get good. Whatever her daddy wanted could wait. Knowing him, he'd had her stepmother call with another blind date Mabel Ann would have to politely decline.

The phone buzzed, buzzed, and buzzed again, causing Mabel Ann to lose her train of thought, and her temper. Not unusual for the "ice queen" of the Zapata Pack.

"Where is it, dammit," she grumbled, searching her enormous bag for the ridiculously small cell phone.

Why did she have so much stuff? Mabel Ann always liked a big bag. They were great for lugging along her eReader, work laptop, and even paper-

backs when the mood struck her. The problem was it ended up becoming her dumping ground for things she didn't want to deal with.

Notes from her father. Mail she didn't feel like reading. And pesky notices from the Pack that she was due to submit to a *sniff and mate* test. Okay, so technically that wasn't what it was called.

It was simply a compatibility test for true mates given in close proximity and with a lot less clothing than she thought necessary for such a thing. The two Pack mates would strip, shift, sniff, and if they were amenable, or if the Fates came down and zapped their asses, they would mate.

Her she-Wolf snarled at the idea of having to be sniffed. No way. She would not submit to that kind of humiliation. If her mate was somewhere in the Pack, she'd have found him by now.

"Aha!" she announced grabbing the thing.

"Afternoon Mabel Ann," Georgie Smith called out from down the lane.

The long-legged she-Wolf was tall and thin, and prettier than a fresh daisy. She came strolling by near every day to have a chat with Mabel, seeing as how they were bosom buddies since preschool.

"Afternoon," she said, trying to open the silly gadget that was still buzzing like mad.

"Here," Georgie said with a slow smile.

That infinite patience of hers was said to pay off in the bedroom if the local boys could be believed, but Mabel never had the guts to ask. Still, she had dry hands and knew everything about the shorter, plumper Wolf, including her passwords. There was no one else in the whole Pack Mabel Ann trusted more.

"Thanks."

"Well, you're about ten minutes late to the party," Georgie said and nodded towards the men and women who'd left their shops and pulled their cars over to chat excitedly with one another.

"Well, what's going on?" Mabel asked, not bothering to read the email.

"Alpha Garra just sent an all pack alert. Seems we're gonna have a High Alpha again."

"No! They finally decided. Well, it's about time," Mabel Ann growled, her she-Wolf rising up quicker than the tide.

Her inner beast had been growing more unruly with every passing day. Nothing like what the staid librarian was used to. Their current Alpha had only risen to his position a few years ago, and he was so busy trying to placate his mate with trips to Dallas and San Anton, he'd been unaware of the difficult time his own Pack was having with all the recent changes.

"Yes, the Council of Shifters, um, the international one, I mean, not the locals, anyway they voted, and there is gonna be a new election," she nodded earnestly.

"And guess what?" she asked, and Mabel was aware she was not going to be finishing her break with chapter thirteen after all.

Sad whine.

"What?" she asked politely.

"They are holding the election here!"

"Wait. What?"

Mabel Ann's mouth opened and closed like a fish out of water. The elections were being held on the Zapata Pack lands.

"But how? Why?"

"Who knows why, sugar? Let's just enjoy it. I mean, can you just imagine all those big, sexy, *foreign* Wolves running around here in their Gucci and Armani," she said, practically vibrating with energy.

"Imagine the conversation," Georgie said with a sigh of longing.

"Sure would be a change from horses and farm equipment," Mabel Ann replied.

Not that it mattered. Even if Georgie was right and all sorts of big city Shifters came to their tiny town to have this all important meeting, Mabel Ann was unlikely to find her match.

After all, who would want a chubby Werewolf who was all bark, no bite?

No, she was so not going down that road again. After her disastrous break up with none other than Santiago Garro, present Alpha of the Zapata Pack, himself back when they were teenagers, Mabel Ann had shied away from men.

It might seem stupid to everyone else, but she'd thought he was the one. Had even almost given him her virginity. She'd had it all planned out. The perfect prom weekend romance.

Except, like many Wolves, Santiago had been an athlete. While away at a championship game in Dallas, he'd had his first shift. And wouldn't you know it, his fated mate was there in the very same hotel where he'd stayed with his team.

He'd shifted back to human, fucked her, gave her his claiming bite, and brought her back to the Zapata Pack lands. At eighteen, they'd been young, but no one could say no to a fated pair.

They were just too rare and special for such a thing. Santiago's run of good luck hadn't stopped

then. The Alpha stepped down amicably, and Santiago, or Sonny, as he was called, rose to Alpha status.

He was young. He was gorgeous. And he was a total asshat, in Mabel Ann's humble opinion. His mate of eight years had given him no pups, and she demanded to return to Dallas every fortnight to see her kin.

What kind of Alpha ran his Pack from a distance of almost five hundred miles every other weekend? It was unconscionable. Now and then, she'd caught Sonny looking at her with those amber eyes she used to love, all big and sad. Like he felt guilty or something about finding his mate.

Why should he? The Fates had their own ideas, and she was not one to stand in their way. Besides, they'd never professed true love to one another. And really, he'd been the only male to pay her any attention back then.

Of course, nowadays with Daddy's fortune taking off, Mabel Ann had prospects coming out the wazoo. All of whom she'd turned down with a firm *no*. She was not the kind of woman to settle. To date she had not participated in even one of the Alpha's *get naked and find your mate tests*. She'd simply refused.

"Oh, by the way Crystal is hosting another *sniff*

and mate event this weekend. She told me to tell you to come."

"Yeah well, unless she uses her Alpha voice on me, I am not going, Georgie."

"You say that, but maybe it's not a bad idea, Mabel Ann. I mean, I'm not getting any younger either," her best friend replied.

She had to be out of her mind. Not only was Georgie tall, and thin, with killer legs and even deadlier grin, she was a dominant she-Wolf and very much in demand. From her platinum locks to her plump red lips, baby doll blue eyes, and impossibly thick lashes, the woman was drop dead gorgeous.

Truth was, if Mabel Ann was not besties with Georgie, she'd have to hate her guts. No one was that perfect. Except, Georgie really was. Movie star gorgeous, and nicer and kinder than Mother Teresa.

How am I supposed to get a mate when Georgie is still single?

Georgie was saying her goodbyes when Mabel Ann's phone rang. That was the only reason she'd forgotten to look down at the device before answering it, and she could have cursed herself for her stupidity the second Bonny's voice sounded in her ear.

"Mabel Ann, this is the fourth time I called you this morning alone," Bonny said, and not for the first time, Mabel Ann wondered how anyone could sound so nasal and high-pitched at the same time.

"Now, your daddy had a meeting with the Alpha today, and our Alpha fem is arranging a mate testing before this whole to do happens that High Alpha business," she said.

"Bonny, I am telling you, just like I told my Daddy, and Crystal. I will not submit to a test to find my mate. If it happens, it happens, but I am perfectly fine remaining unmated—"

"Oh, you don't mean that, Mabel Ann, but if it's your weight, honey, I found this new alchemist down in Starr County, and he says he can make the pounds come off just like that!"

The woman went on and on, but she did not hear a word. Mabel Ann was too busy trying to rein in her suddenly very pissed off she-Wolf.

OMG! She did not just go there.

It was no good. Her temper flared to life and Mabel Ann squeezed the cell phone so hard it crushed in her hands. Darn it. That was the third one in two months. Dropping the useless hunk back inside her bag, she closed her book and returned to her duties.

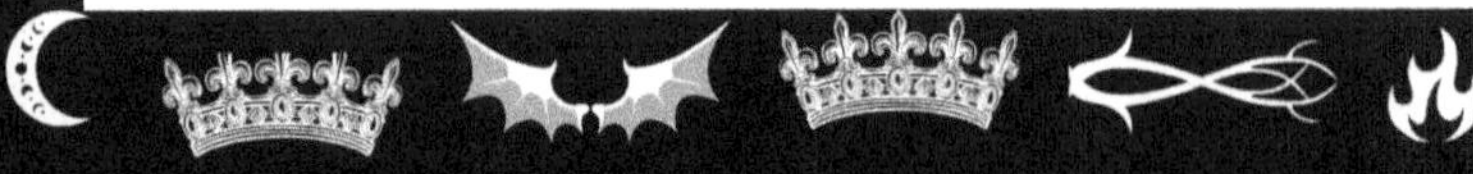

As head librarian, she was in charge of a substantial number of things, including acquiring new books. Today was the day the catalogs were updated, and she always looked forward to going through the offerings.

Shaking her head, she pushed all the petty things that annoyed her out of her mind. It wasn't her fault this Pack was stuck somewhere in the previous century. But one thing was certain, Mabel Ann did not need any male to make her feel complete or valuable.

She was a woman of worth. Intelligent, dedicated, hardworking, and pretty too. She might not be thin, but as her beloved late mother used to say, skinny was not everything.

Mabel Ann had plenty to offer the right man. But what she really wanted was someone worthy of her. Someone with plenty to offer on his own. Why should she settle because she did not fit society' standard of beauty?

The heck with all that. Mabel Ann did not suffer from a lack of self-confidence. She might still be a virgin, but that was her choice. Sighing, she looked back at the paperback copy of the paranormal romance from a local indie author she'd been reading.

Hard to believe a human could get it so right, she thought and shook her head. Pack politics were one thing. She trusted her father and the Alpha to do their best when it came to this High Alpha business. But as far as intricacies of the heart were considered, Mabel Ann would follow her own instincts.

"There will be no *sniff and mate* nonsense for me," she muttered.

"What did you say Miss Williams?" Jimmy, a teenager who worked parttime in the library asked.

He was loading the heavy, wheeled cart they used to restock the returns a few feet away from her. But since he was a Werewolf too, Jimmy heard her clear as day.

"Nothing Jimmy," she said, offering the boy a smile.

The skinny teen nodded his head and went back to doing what he was doing. Not a lot of teenagers hung around the library, but Jimmy had always liked to read. Too bad he wasn't older, she thought with a rueful grin.

"If you ever need to talk, Miss Williams, I am here for you," he offered quietly before pushing the cart towards the aisles.

"Thank you, Jimmy. I'm fine," she said, and winked.

"If I don't see you later, have a good night."

"You too."

Mabel Ann grinned and went back to work. There were only a few hours left till closing and she had a slew of books to order. She paused going through the self-help section.

Snorting a little, she pondered ordering a few dating guides and relationship books. The scandal that would cause!

She could see the Alpha now, storming in her library to tear down her display. She was not going to do it, of course. That would embarrass Sassy, and she loved her old man even if his new mate was a bit hard to take.

"I just don't want you to be alone, Mabel Ann."

She understood the sentiment. After all, who wanted to be alone? But her father, the Alpha, and his mate, all needed to understand one thing. Mabel Ann had standards.

Wolf males, in her opinion, were so damn macho. Always showing off for their females, like they were still in high school. Hell, Jimmy was more mature than any of them. The teenager was highly sensitive, well read, and more thoughtful than any of the adult males in the whole Pack.

Not that she was into robbing cradles. She was

just saying. At least there was hope for the future females of the Zapata Pack. As far as Mabel Ann was concerned, she would simply have to be satisfied with book boyfriends and her Bob, her battery operated boyfriend.

Things could be worse.

Read more here: https://www.cdgorri.com/books/werewolf-fever

MEET THE MOTLEY CREWD SHIFTERS!

Once upon a time...

Nah, scratch that.

These aren't those kinds of stories.

Yeah, there are supernatural creatures, magic, and love inside these tales. But there's also crude behavior, foul language, and steamy sex scenes, involving boorish alpha males with bad attitudes and over the top possessive behavior.

Still wanna stick around?

Excellent!

Now, we have all heard there are more things in this universe than you or I *or anyone* truly knows.

Well, this group of supernatural misfits is testing the limits of what they know in order to chase the one thing they never thought they'd have a shot at controlling...*their destinies.*

But only the Fates can determine true love, and in Barren County, New Jersey, these Urban Cowboy Shifters are going to find out the hard way. Sometimes it's not about the family you were born into. Sometimes it's about the family you choose. Or in this case, *the Crew.*

Meet our Cowboys:
Maximillian Leeds
Emmet Quinn
Dante Bianco
Kian O'Malley
Zeke Gordon

**This is a series of interconnected paranormal romance standalones with steamy scenes, foul language, crude behavior, plus size heroines, mating rituals, claiming bites, possessive book boyfriends, HEA endings, raunchy humor and more.*

*VISIT THE MOTLEY CREWD SHIFTERS
SERIES PAGE*

Hearts of Stone Series

Shifter City

Will her love break through his heart of stone?

Shifter Village

Are memories enough to warm his frozen heart?

Shifter Scrooge

Can her holiday spirit unlock his icy heart?

Shifter CEO

He's a hardhearted CEO, but he needs her help...

ALSO BY C.D. GORRI

Paranormal Romance Books:

Macconwood Pack Novel Series:

Macconwood Pack Tales Series:

The Falk Clan Tales:

The Bear Claw Tales:

The Barvale Clan Tales:

Barvale Holiday Tales:

Purely Paranormal Romance Books:

The Wardens of Terra:

The Maverick Pride Tales:

Dire Wolf Mates:

Wyvern Protection Unit:

Jersey Sure Shifters/EveL Worlds:

The Guardians of Chaos:

Twice Mated Tales

Hearts of Stone Series

Moongate Island Tales

Mated in Hope Falls

Speed Dating with the Denizens of the Underworld

Hungry Fur Love

Island Stripe Pride

Motley Crewd Shifters

<u>NYC Shifter Tales</u>

A Howlin' Good Fairytale Retelling

<u>Witch Shifter Clan</u>

<u>Lords of Nightfall</u>

<u>When Worlds Collide</u>

Young Adult/Urban Fantasy Books

The Grazi Kelly Novel Series

The Angela Tanner Files

G'Witches Magical Mysteries Series

Co-written with P. Mattern

Witches of Westwood Academy

with Gina Kincade

Blackthorn Academy For Supernaturals

Be sure to check out my BUY DIRECT BUNDLES and get 30% off when you buy available only my website.

Click here for The Official C.D. Gorri Reading List - free

download

****

<u>Contemporary Romance Books:</u>

<u>Cherry On Top Tales</u>

Her Yule His Log

His Carrot Her Muffin

Her Chocolate His Bar

His Pickle Her Jam

Her Trick His Treat

His Wood Her Fire

Her Birthday His Package

<u>Wild Billionaire Romance</u>

His Wild Obsession

His Wild Temptation

His Wild Seduction

His Wild Attraction

**Bonus Scene His Wild Halloween Night*

<u>Jersey Bad Boys</u>

Merciful Lies

Devious Lies

Pitiful Lies

Mergers & Acquisitions

Desperate Measures

Desperate Needs

Desperate Desires

Desperate Actions

Carolina Rugby Romance

A Reason To Try

The Break Down

***

About the Author

USA Today Bestselling Author C.D. Gorri writes steamy Paranormal & Contemporary Romance and Urban Fantasy packed with heart, humor, and heat.

Join her mailing list here: https://www.cdgorri.com/newsletter

A lifelong book lover, she's rarely without a story in hand, and her own tales reflect that passion. Based in her beloved New Jersey, C.D. weaves the Garden State into many of her stories, grounding even the wildest supernatural adventures with a touch of home.

Her books are fast-paced, full of feels, and always end with a satisfying HEA. You'll meet sassy, curvy heroines and the possessive, love-driven heroes who adore them, whether they're Shifters, Vampires,

Witches, or just morally gray men falling hard in her contemporary worlds.

If you're into fated mates, fierce love, and action-packed romance where loyalty wins and love always triumphs then *welcome*. You're in the right place.

Thanks for reading!

Del mare alla stella,

C.D. Gorri

Curvy Heroines & Epic Heroes for the avid reader.

http://www.cdgorri.com

https://www.facebook.com/Cdgorribooks

https://www.bookbub.com/authors/c-d-gorri

https://twitter.com/cgor22

https://instagram.com/cdgorri/

https://www.goodreads.com/cdgorri

https://www.tiktok.com/@cdgorriauthor